Knight

A Chess Club Mystery - Book Two

TK Eldridge

Graffridge Publishing

Cover by Lizzie Dunlap of PixieCovers.com

Editing by Donna A. Martz of MartzProofing.com

Contents

For Donna, because none of this would exist without you.

When push comes to shove, you always know who to turn to. That being a family isn't a social construct but an instinct. – Jodi Picoult, author

Chapter One

Milos Owens tossed the last report onto the pile and leaned back against the leather padding. The failure of the operation in Lakeridge still stung and the loss of so much product and money had cost him a couple of good operatives. There was no mercy when millions of credits worth of designer drugs ended up in the storage facilities of the Federal Bureau of Investigation and Security. He'd had no qualms about shoving the two men out of the heli half a mile above the Pisgah National Forest.

He did feel a little sorry for the crew he'd sent to find the bodies and bury them, but only because it had been his temper that had caused him to shove Nelson and Cragan out over the mountains instead of waiting for the lake where they wouldn't have needed to be found and buried.

Milos's gaze shifted to the windows that looked out across the Potomac to where the Washington Monument gleamed in the evening light. A tap on the door didn't pull his gaze away from the view. "Come in."

"Mr. Owens, a Mr. Samuels is here to see you. He doesn't have an appointment." The voice of his assistant was calm and clear, but when he turned, he could see the flicker of fear in Amanda Michaels' eyes.

"Send him in, Amanda, then you can leave for the evening," he told her, then slowly got to his feet and went to the bar. He poured himself two fingers of an exquisite Macallan and took a sip as the door closed, then opened again.

"Are you going to offer me any?" Jonas Samuels asked as he entered the room. Mahogany paneling gleamed beneath original paintings and bordered glass shelves with awards, trophies, and framed photos of the man in front of him beside several world leaders. It was the view of the city beyond the one wall of glass that was the focal point of the room, however. A reminder that the man that sat behind the desk controlled much of what went on in that city.

And what he didn't control, Samuels liked to think he did.

Jonas looked at Milos and had to appreciate the presentation. The man's hair had gone silver from the blonde it had once been and his eyes were a crystalline blue in a pale face of angles and planes. A designer suit in soft gray gave Milos Owens a deceptively approachable look with the pale blue shirt, the collar opened. Jonas was a direct contrast to Milos in appearance. His dusky skin, dark eyes, and thick dark hair in tight curls at the top hid his age that was about ten years older than Milos's fifty-six, but Jonas looked younger than his years and Milos looked older. They even wore the same designer, but Jonas opted for a black suit and gray shirt. He felt it made him look more intimidating.

"I could pour you a whiskey," Milos said. "But I don't think you'll be staying long enough to enjoy it, Jonas."

"The new facility in Lake County is not yet finished. That's holding up production and needs to be addressed," Jonas said as he settled onto a leather Chesterfield sofa. "The board has asked me to come speak to you and find out when production will be back up to Univy standards."

Milos arched one silvered brow, then ran a hand through the thick silver curls he kept fashionably trimmed. "Univy's standards are *my* standards, Jonas. With the FBIS interest in Lake County, circumspect behavior is more conducive to long term business goals than a speedy spin-up of production." He leaned back against the desk and folded his arms, the glass of whiskey forgotten at the bar for the moment.

"The board -" Jonas started to say and Milos held up one hand, palm out.

"The board answers to me," Milos said. "I can always go private again and eliminate the need for the board."

"The board could easily expose the various less-than-legal enterprises Univy has in process, too. Mutually assured destruction," Jonas said. "With the purchase of DESCO, people are watching Univy and looking to see if we front ourselves a private army. You know they always want to take down the biggest kid on the playground."

"I'm well aware," Milos said. "And I'm handling everything. The board is just there to look good and soak up profits. Tell them to take a breath and let me do what I do best."

"And what is that?" Jonas asked.

Milos picked up his glass and gave Jonas a cold smile. "Run the world."

Chapter Two

Chasen Templeton Payne decided he needed to seriously reconsider some of his life choices. It was early morning, and he was in his truck as it sat in the parking lot behind the Lakeridge County sheriff's office. It was a Monday, so he'd grabbed coffee for himself and a box of mixed pastries to bring into the office as a way to sweeten his arrival as the Fucking New Guy.

He'd not been the FNG in a long, long time – and he'd never been the FNG in his hometown. All of this conspired to make him wonder what in the actual hell he was doing with his life that had brought him to this particular set of circumstances.

Yes, logically, he knew he was here because when your chosen family asks you to come help, you show up. He didn't really have anything holding him in Raleigh, and a change of venue had, at the time, looked like a brilliant solution to his issues.

Now? Now he wasn't so sure.

"Just suck it up, Chase, and get your ass in gear," he said to himself. "But first, a donut." He picked out a jelly filled and took a bite, then washed the sugar down with a swallow of coffee. Of course, that's the exact moment when Lieutenant Cassidy Redbird walked in front of his truck, stopped, then turned to stare at him through the windshield.

He pictured what she saw – a big black man with a shaved head, trimmed moustache and goatee now covered with powdered sugar. His suitcoat and collared shirt gave him a professional appearance – if you discounted the sugar dusting.

What he saw? A gorgeous woman with legs for miles, dressed in slacks, low-heeled boots, and a jacket that nipped in at the waist and flared over her hips. She had tawny skin, wide dark eyes, and silky black hair cut to chin length that slid across her jawline when she tipped her head. Then she smiled and Chase's heart stuttered. Sure, he'd seen a picture of the woman, but in person? Her charisma and sense of presence knocked the wind out of him.

Cassidy arched one slender brow, then gave a soft laugh and approached his driver side door. A tap on the window and he lowered it with the hand he'd been using to brush the sugar off of himself. She hoped he didn't expect her to shake hands now.

"Lieutenant Redbird," Chase said as the window sank out of the way. Damn, now he could smell the faintest hint of some light fragrance as the breeze fluttered the ends of her hair.

"Detective Payne, correct?" Cassidy replied.

"That's correct," Chase replied. "I was just fortifying myself before I came inside. Want a donut?"

"Sure," Cassidy said and when Chase held out the box, she picked a Boston Cream and wrapped it in a napkin. "The minute those hit the break room table, they'll be gone. Appreciate you letting me grab one first. I'll see you inside?"

"Soon as I wipe the sugar off of myself," Chase grinned. "I'll put the box in the break room and stop in at Personnel, then come by your office."

"I'm not your boss, Detective," Cassidy reminded him. "Not yet, anyway."

"And I'm not your boss, Lieutenant," Chase said with a smile. "Not yet, anyway."

"May the best candidate win," Cassidy said with a wink, then turned away to head inside.

Chase made no secret of the fact he watched her hips sway as she crossed the small lot. He then finished up his donut, brushed off the fresh dusting of sugar, and grabbed his gear to follow her. The challenge in Cassidy's eyes had fired him up. He would be the Chief – or he'd be the Assistant Chief. Either way, he would be in a better situation than he'd been in Raleigh.

His day was already looking up.

Cassidy put down her coffee and the donut on her desk, then stowed her things and sat in her chair. Her fingerprint opened up her computer and sent the clear plate of screen to rise up from the slot in the desk so it hovered at eye level. The system scrolled her daily feed and schedule across the surface while she checked the location of the team of cops that worked for the town of Lakeridge, North Carolina.

The previous chief had been arrested, as had his son, the assistant chief – and now with the Halsteads out of the way, those two seats were open. She knew the chances of her making chief were slim, but she was going to give it her best shot because she knew she was one of the top choices. She would've said *the* top choice – before Chase Payne came back to town. The file she'd put together on him was impressive, but there were questions and a couple of gaps that were, she'd been told, due to his working cases that had been kept under wraps.

It wasn't Cassidy's style to try and play those gaps into negative angles she could use to push him out of contention, but after working under the Halsteads for a few years, the idea of using every tool available had been her first thought. Then she took a breath and decided if she wanted a department that wasn't an echo of the twisted, criminal behavior that it had suffered under Chief Bernstrom Halstead Sr. and his son, Assistant Chief Byron Halstead, then it was time to try and think more like a good cop and less like a cop in survival mode.

A tap at her door brought her gaze up from the screen to meet the smile of Sergeant Ellery Adler. "Come on in, Adler. What can I do for you this morning?"

"Morning, LT. I grabbed a couple of donuts from the box Detective Payne brought in and thought you might want one," Elle said as she held out a blueberry filled pastry. Elle's long dark hair was braided up and twisted into a knot at the back of her neck – exactly how Cassidy had worn hers until a couple of years ago when she'd cut it all off. Ellery's tan-hued skin, high cheekbones, and slender nose spoke of their shared Cherokee ancestry, while Cassidy's eyes were nearly black and Elle's eyes were the gray of Irish storm clouds. Strangers had mistaken them for sisters, but it was more likely they picked up on the way they both moved like cops.

Cassidy chuckled and picked up the Boston Cream that sat on the napkin on her desk. "I caught one in the parking lot, but thanks for thinking of me."

Elle dropped into a chair at the corner of Cassidy's desk and sighed. "We can split it? Because if I try and take it back there, it'll be like throwing raw meat into a tank of piranha. And if I don't split it with you, I'll eat it all myself and that'd be bad."

Cassidy chuckled and caught Elle's wink. "Sure, we can split it. Then I won't feel guilty either." She took a sip of her coffee, then did something she'd sworn she'd *not* do this morning. "Tell me about Chase Payne." Knowing that Elle lived next door to the man, she hoped she could gain some insight on him.

"What do you want to know?" Elle asked around a mouthful of donut. "He's one of the Chess Club crew. Chase, along with my Grant – as well as Zach Hawthorne, Logan McMann, Mykal Cutler, and the late Wes Davenport all bonded in high school as members of the chess club. They're as much family to each other as if they shared blood."

Cassidy gave a wink. "*Your* Grant?" she teased, then she shook her head and sent the silky strands of hair bouncing. "Huh. I didn't know that they'd all met in the chess club. I knew they'd been friends from high school, from reading the files on the Davenport murder," Cassidy replied.

"Did you see the file on Alexander Layton's murder from nearly sixteen years ago?" Elle asked. "He was the teacher that ran the club. When he was murdered, they all scattered. All except Wes Davenport."

"And Payne ended up in the Triangle and distinguished himself as a good cop with solid instincts and then as one of the state's top homicide detectives," Cassidy said. "Now he's here. Why?"

Elle paused mid-chew, then washed the bite down with coffee. "Because of Wes's murder being unsolved and his need to be home." She knew damned well that wasn't the whole reason, but that was all she was willing – or able – to share.

"I guess that's a good reason," Cassidy said. "Just feels like there should be more."

Elle gave a shrug. "Well, you came home to take care of your pops and left a promising career in Nashville. Sometimes, home is just where you need to be."

"Good point," Cassidy replied. "Okay, Sergeant. Take your half of the donut and get to work. We all have a stack of files to get through before we can be sure the Halsteads didn't leave us any nasty surprises."

"On it, LT," Elle said as she handed over half of the blueberry filled donut and headed out of the office.

Cassidy took a bite of the pastry and stared at her screen. It was going to take a while to get through the mess

the Halsteads had left behind. Months – maybe years.
Cassidy settled in to dig.

Chapter Three

Wes sat on the roof of Myke's place and watched Grant, Chase, Myke, and Elle kick the soccer ball back and forth, aiming for the makeshift goals Chase had set up in the road. The light was fading, but the glow from the road lights gave them enough illumination to play a little bit longer.

Laughter and the soft grunts of bodies colliding made Wes miss his physical body more than he had in a long time. Long being relative since he'd only been dead a few months. Being a ghost meant he couldn't appreciate the rich scents of pine from the forest and the fragrance of the flowers planted around the small homes. Each one had been created exactly the same, then modified to fit the individual living there.

Myke's place was the first on the left when you came over the bridge from Red's parking area, then Ellery's place next to Myke, and Chase on the other side of Elle.

Across the road from Chase would be Logan's place and then Zach's up behind his. Grant had moved in with Ellery while they worked on getting their home built on some Adler family land he'd purchased for that purpose.

It made him happy to see his friends together once more. It'd be better if Zach and Logan were there, too, but he'd heard they were coming back as soon as they'd wrapped up a few things. Did it bother him that they were only back because he'd been murdered? Maybe a little.

Honestly, he was just glad they were back – and that it was turning out to be a positive thing for all of them so far. Now if they could just figure out who had killed him.

He was pretty sure he knew the why. That Master Key he'd been working on would shift global power the minute it went live. He felt a bit guilty for creating it, if he were being honest with himself. The risks were enormous – but the benefits were enormous, too. Sure, the Key could've caused chaos – but in a time of crisis, it would've saved lives. It would've allowed a shuttle to be taken over remotely and landed if the pilot was unable to fly, or increased the water filtration processes for a city or town if a toxin spilled into a stream. It would also have allowed someone to shut down the filtration for a city from an off-planet location, or crash a shuttle across the world. Location didn't matter, as long as it was connected to the network.

Should one not create something simply because it could be used in evil ways? Something to ponder as he watched his friends play.

Chase sprawled in the chair on his screen porch, feet up on an ottoman, cold beer in his hand. "Okay, I'll confess. I love the new furniture, Grant," he said to his friend that sat across from him on the outdoor couch, one arm around Ellery. He also had to admit they looked good together. Elle's dark, slender beauty and Grant's red-brown curls and pale skin made an attractive contrast, but it was the pure love and adoration they showed each other that really struck him. He wanted that for himself, but had never found it. He didn't think he ever would. Who would risk partnering with a cop like him?

"You mean you're finally coming around to the realization that torn up camp chairs suck?" Grant teased.

"Yeah, they suck. But when you move often, or don't really spend any time at your apartment, it's not a priority, y'know?" Chase replied.

Myke opened the screen door and slipped inside, a bag in one hand. "Sandwiches, courtesy of the future Mayor Foster. She also sent up a berry pie." Mykal's sable-hued skin stretched over sharp cheekbones, a slender nose, and narrow jawline. Her full lips and wide brown eyes were expressive and softened the edgy haircut of medium brown tousled curls with light purple streaks at the top, and the sides and back shaved to stubble. Her body was lean and not what one would consider curvy, with long legs and expressive hands.

Chase got to his feet first and took the bag from Myke to unpack it on the table against one wall of the screen porch. "Miz Lacey already had my vote, she didn't need to bake a pie to cement the deal."

"Mayor Mom is still the same mom," Grant said. "Just with some excitement around the coming election."

Italian cold-cut subs were drawn out of the bag and laid out on the table next to a pie that Chase could feel was still warm. "Food from her hands is always exceptional," he told his friends. "I'm just appreciative as fuck that she thinks of all of us."

"She doesn't have any competition for the mayoral seat right now, and it's almost too late to slide another candidate in, so she'll get it," Ellery said.

"Here's hoping," Myke replied. "Oh, Grant – a package came for you down at the gate, so I ran it through the scanner and brought it up." She gave Chase a smile. "I think it's your drone."

"Where'd you leave it?" Grant asked.

"On your porch. It looks like rain is moving in, so I didn't want to leave it on the step," Myke replied.

"I'll go get it," Grant said. "I know Chase is eager to get this thing going."

Chase sat down with a sandwich and his beer. "We need to see if there are any other maglev spurs that have popped up around Lakeridge, first. Then we need to scan county-wide. I don't believe the one by Elle's parent's place was the only one Univy slid in under the wire."

"I have to admit it was pretty slick of them to drop a spur right where they were manufacturing the drugs," Elle said after she swallowed a bit of her sandwich. "And it's too slick for the Halsteads to have thought of it."

Myke shook her head. "The Halsteads weren't complete idiots, but they didn't have the resources to do that kind of work as quickly and as quietly as it was done. That smacks of major financial and material backing – and we've already started to hone our sights in on Univy."

"Particularly since they bought out DESCO," Chase said. "Now they've got their own private army."

The screen door banged as Grant returned.

"This drone isn't going to be able to scan the whole county for you," Grant said as he came back inside with the box. "That's too much land to cover. However, we've got a couple of personal helis between here and Ma's that I could be helping you get your certifications on." He gave Chase a wink and set the box down.

"Wait, I thought every cop had to be heli certified..." Elle started, then caught herself. "Ohh, right. Plausible deniability. I get it now."

Chase leaned over and watched as Grant pulled the X-4k drone out of the box and set it on the floor. "That's a thing of beauty," he murmured.

"You bet it is," Grant replied. "Best drone out there. It's fast, light, durable, can carry five times it's weight before it starts to slow down the response time, and has a lens system that can show the pollen on a bee's ass from over a mile up."

"We're going to have fun with this," Chase said. "It'll be even more fun if we manage to catch the bad guys doing stupid shit."

"That's your job, isn't it?" Grant teased as he hooked up the power pack to a charger base. "Let's tuck this to the side and cover it up while it's charging. That pie isn't going to eat itself and there's nothing we can do until it's juiced."

Elle paused before she took another bite and arched a brow at Grant. "You really think someone is going to come up here and see that thing? The only ones that live up here are us – and they'd have to get past Red Jefferson's security system to reach us."

"Better to not take any chances. We're not the only ones that can get a drone," Chase said.

A sheet of protective wrap from the packaging made a good cover for the drone and they settled down to eat. As the conversation flowed around him, Chase kept looking over at the lump under the cover. If he could find solid evidence that Univy was breaking the law in his town or county, it'd be one step closer to getting justice for Alex Layton – and for Wes.

Chapter Four

"I've got to get going, Doda," Cassidy said as she leaned in to kiss her father's cheek. He'd rallied back from the heart attack that had brought her back to Lakeridge to care for him. It had been a few difficult years and a lot of rehabilitation, but Sid was fully independent once more. Cassidy could have moved out – but why would she? They took care of each other and the sprawling five-bedroom home was more than large enough for the two of them to stay out of each other's way when alone time was needed.

Sid Redbird reached up a hand and patted her arm. "Stay safe. I'm going to tend the garden after the news. I'll do venison steaks on the grill tonight when you get home, yeah?"

"Sounds good. I don't expect to be late, but you know how it is."

"I know how it is, daughter. Don't forget your coffee. I left it on the table by the door."

"Thank you, Doda. Call me if you need anything," Cassidy said as she grabbed the coffee and stepped outside. The views from the front of the house weren't as awe-inspiring as the views from the back – but they were still pretty amazing. The Blue Ridge mountains rose up against a pink-tinged sky as the sun rose on a landscape that could use more than a little rain. Things had been drying out more than usual this early in the season and she hoped they'd get some wet weather soon.

The drive in to work took about fifteen minutes, but it was time Cassidy cherished to get herself in the right headspace to deal with the day. The good mood she had cultivated on the drive disappeared the minute she stepped in through the back entrance of the station and spotted Officer Beauregard Fitch leaning against the wall.

Fitch had dirty blonde hair cut in a military style, a perfectly pressed uniform over a pale, slightly overweight figure, and mud-brown eyes that made a woman feel like she needed a shower with steel wool to get the slimy feeling off of her once that gaze had slid from head to toe. She despised the man, but didn't dare let it show. His father sat on the state law enforcement judiciary panel that determined the internal rules and regulations for all of North Carolina's cops.

"Good mornin', ma'am," Fitch said as Cassidy turned sideways to edge past him. He stepped into her way and smiled as she stopped. "I said – good morning, ma'am."

"Officer Fitch, move," Cassidy hissed through her teeth. "And if you can't use my rank, don't speak to me."

"Yes, ma'am, Lieutenant ma'am. I don't suppose you'd like to join me for lunch today?" Fitch asked as he kept the hallway blocked with his bulk.

She turned to glare at Fitch and gave him an icy smile. "Not if you were the last man on earth. Never mind the fact that it's against policy. Get out of my way, *officer*. Now. That's an order."

Fitch's eyes went dark and he leaned into her as one hand dropped to his pulse weapon. The back entrance door flew open and Chase stepped in. Fitch nearly jumped back when he saw Chase, and Cassidy turned and hurried away. She didn't want to lose her temper with Fitch in front of Chase, and she didn't want to look like she needed Chase to come to her rescue.

Chase arched a brow at Cassidy's rush, then turned to look at Fitch who glared at Chase as if he wanted to spit in his face.

"Problem?" Chase asked.

"None of your concern, boy," Fitch snarled and turned away.

Chase went completely still, then took two steps and snatched Fitch up by the back of his neck and flung him into the wall. He leaned over and glared down at the short, pudgy man. One of his massive arms rested against the wall over Fitch's head and Chase's solid torso blocked him from moving.

"I asked if there was a problem," Chase rumbled. "I guess there just might be. See, I don't think we've been properly introduced. I'm Lieutenant Chasen Payne, recently the top homicide detective in the Triangle area, now come home to clean up the mess those fucking Halsteads left behind." He dropped his gaze to the curve of Fitch's belly, then back up to the pale face now flushed with fury. "Seems like a particularly *small* turd got left behind and needs to be...flushed out. Is that the case, Fitch? You need to be cleaned up?"

"Get off of me," Fitch rasped and pushed at Chase. He might as well have been pushing at the brick wall behind him.

"Watch yourself, Fitch," Chase warned. "I'm going to be keeping an eye on you. Get moving. Your day started twenty minutes ago."

As soon as Chase backed off, Fitch tugged up his pants and lifted his chin. "Better watch yourself as well, *boy*. You don't know who my daddy is."

Chase smiled, but it never reached his eyes. "Well, gol*ly* Massa Fitch. I sure am worried some about whether some fat ass patrol cop's got a big shot daddy." Those dark chocolate eyes lasered in on Fitch and the smile disappeared. "It's Lieutenant to you, asswipe. You need to run to your daddy? Go right ahead. I'll take care of both of you."

Fitch felt the hairs on the back of his neck lift and swore he saw his death in those dark eyes before he turned and scurried out the back door to the lot.

Chase watched him go and let out a huff of breath. Some people never did learn and he was sure that Fitch was just one of the many he'd have to deal with now that he was back.

He'd been at his desk for about an hour before the call came in. A couple that had been hiking out of Pisgah National Forest had found a shallow grave, disturbed by local wildlife. They'd called it in to the closest ranger station and went back to the trail so as to guide in the ranger that responded. That ranger had called it in to Pinehurst, who had in turn called in Lakeridge as it was just on the edge of the town border. As the head homicide guy, it was handed to Chase – so he grabbed his kit bag and headed out to the site.

He pulled into the parking area and noted that the coroner's van and a couple of patrol cars had already arrived. One officer was keeping the curious back behind the tape and he gave the man a nod as he tapped his wrist device against the log box. A beep sounded and he ducked under the tape and started up the trail.

It had been years since Chase had found himself on the hiking trails around Lake County. He had once been a regular, and the scents and sounds brought the memories rushing back. Time spent with his father, walking through these trees, pausing to fish, then setting up camp and cooking what they'd caught. Those memories scattered when he caught the scent of old blood and freshly uncovered decay.

The scene had been taped off well outside the body location, for which he was grateful. Nothing worse than trying to work a scene that everyone and their brother had traipsed all over.

"Lieutenant Payne," he said to the officer on the perimeter. The young woman gave him a nod, then called it in to the officer in charge before she lifted the tape for him to duck under. "Ranger Belfleur and Sergeant Williams are about ten yards up the trail, Lieutenant."

"Thank you, Officer," Chase replied as he walked the trail, his gaze tracking the area around him. He paused and looked up at a spot about ten feet from the trail where the canopy of branches had been opened up to the sky. Broken limbs and crushed undergrowth showed where something had crashed through. He made a note of it on his wrist device and marked the coordinates before he moved on to meet up with the sergeant and ranger.

"Lieutenant Payne, I'm Sergeant Angela Williams with Pinehaven PD. We're grateful you could get here so quickly." Her dark blonde hair was pulled back into a short ponytail and her brown eyes snapped with quiet fury. "The body is through there – you can see the drag marks." She half-turned to the ranger. "Don't have to be a tracker to know that it was dragged to the gravesite, then half-assed buried." With her hands on curvy hips, Williams glared at the ranger and Chase got a flash of a very annoyed schoolmarm.

"An animal could've done it," Ranger Belfleur replied. His skin was weathered from the outdoors, but Chase thought the man would've been tanned permanently even if he had an office job. Dark hair cut short and shot with gray gave him a military appearance but it was the flat look in his dark eyes that made Chase pause before he spoke.

"Do you honestly believe an animal dragged the body and dug a grave?" Chase asked him.

"It's possible," Belfleur argued. "We don't need the trails shut down because some idiot got turned into critter kibble."

Chase let out a slow breath, then turned to the markers that led into the trees. "How about you let the homicide specialist determine that, hmm? Stay here, I'll be back in a bit." He watched every step, where he put his feet, where others had put theirs, before he came to the gravesite.

One look and he knew this hastily dug grave had been done by humans. It was squared off at the corners and only about three feet deep. Then there was the body. It had once likely been a man, based off of the tailored suit and Italian loafers, but it'd take the coroner to fully determine. He crouched down and with one gloved hand, reached into the back pocket where a tell-tale lump resided. A Moroccan leather wallet spilled into his hand, and fell open to reveal the ID for a Carl Nelson of Reston, Virginia. A credit chip for National Bank was right in front, but the man's wrist device was not on what remained of either arm. He got to his feet and backtracked to the trail, then started to give orders. He would have a team searching from the site where he saw the broken branches, all the way to here and then in a widening ring around the body. Animals had been at poor Carl's corpse and they could've dragged the wrist device and other valuable clues far from the burial spot. Equipment and people would be all over this area before he would call it done. He'd be tapping Lakeridge and Pinehaven PDs as well as the ranger station for manpower.

It was going to be a long day.

Chapter Five

Cassidy met Ellery in the parking lot after work. She leaned against her vehicle and sighed. "I should get home and check on my father."

"He's doing well now, right? Prefers to have his evening meal with the guys at the pub over a few games of darts?" Elle replied. "Come on, Cassie. You've not done anything fun since you got here, and I promise you, an evening at Redmond Jefferson's, when Lacey Foster is cooking, is going to be worth it."

"I suppose I could come by for an hour or so," Cassidy said. "I mean, she's going to be the mayor, and good relations with the mayor are always something to encourage."

Ellery rolled her eyes and looped her arm through Cassidy's. "For once, stop thinking about work. Just come have a good meal and play a few board games. It's private, so no one will see you relax. Your reputation is safe."

Cassidy gave a soft snort of amusement and shook her head. "My reputation as a ball-busting bitch, you mean? Yeah, that didn't help when Bobo Fitch blocked me in the hallway."

"That sack of lard?" Elle leaned into Cassidy. "Want me to go put muscle liniment in his shorts?"

Cassidy laughed and leaned back once more. "Chase came in and I took advantage of his distracting Bo to get gone. I guess Chase really ruffled Bo's feathers because he was pissy all day long."

"Bo's always pissy," Elle said and tugged Cassidy's arm. "Come on. Get in your car and follow me. We'll stop at my place to change. I know you keep a couple of spare outfits in your car."

"Okay," Cassidy said. "I'll follow you. Let's go."

The two SUV style vehicles were similar in style but Elle's was black and Cassidy's was silver. It was good on the mountain roads and had enough space for gear bags and tools that every cop kept near to hand, so it was a popular type of vehicle in the area. It also meant Cassidy had to pay attention and keep her thoughts from wandering. Wouldn't do to end up following the wrong person because she got distracted. A cop, trained to notice details and stay focused, would never live that one down. Okay, so she'd never let *herself* live that one down.

Ellery was right. She didn't do much in the way of fun, and that needed to change. Cassidy used to have fun – when she was in Nashville. But that was the before time. Before her father needed heart surgery and recuperation time. Before she left everything behind to come home and care for him. Everything, including Everett Lansing, the man she thought she'd end up partnered with for life.

She didn't want to think about all of that now – she just wanted to let herself enjoy a meal with friends.

The sensor on Ellery's car opened the gate and they both drove through and up the winding drive that led to Redmond Jefferson's house. The stone and wood structure took full advantage of the mountain views available from the wide windows where the house sat on the mountain ridge. There was a wide area for parking and another road that wound past the house, across a bridge over Bear Creek, and up through more trees that led to what they all called The Village. A cluster of small homes where a good portion of Red's chosen family lived.

Cassidy followed Ellery's car across the bridge and up to a small house with flowering shrubs and vegetables in raised beds out front, and a strange looking balcony on top of the screen porch.

"This is really cute," Cassidy said as she got out of her vehicle. "They're all the same, but with differences that show the character of the people that live in them."

"I really love being here, but I'm excited about the house Grant and I are building next to my folks," Ellery said as she led the way inside. "Grant's probably already down at Red's, but I need to get out of my uniform. If you want to change out of your suit, the bathroom is right there."

Cassidy hefted the go bag in her hands. "I've got jeans and sneakers in here. I'll only need a minute." She admired the space she could see as she changed her clothes and folded her slacks and jacket into the bag, then added her boots. The sleeveless silk blouse in a soft rose color worked just as well with her jeans as it did the suit, and the color brightened her complexion and helped to hide some of the weariness from the day. She shook out her hair, touched up her lip gloss, and carried the bag back out to the vehicle.

She leaned back against the hatch and let the quiet and the scent of flowers and pine trees wash over her. Her gaze slid to the house she'd been told belonged to Chase. A row of shrubs grew between the two structures, but he didn't have buckets of flowers outside, or even curtains at the windows. Just blinds that were pulled down and a basic mat outside the front door.

"He's not been around enough to do much with his place yet," Elle said as she came back out. "He spends most of his time in Red's gym or at work."

"Y'all even have your own gym out here? That's convenient. And lucky."

"It's been good for all of us, and a way for Red to keep us safe. He's Uncle Red to everyone now, and I think he really enjoys that. Speaking of which, let's head down. I'll ride with you and come back up with Grant later."

Food and laughter were exactly what Cassidy needed. It also allowed her to see Chase outside of their work environment and while she liked who he was both in and out of the office, she could see there was something that he held back from even these people. People he considered family.

He'd arrived late and came down from his place freshly showered and changed into jeans, t-shirt, and sneakers. Lacey had kept a plate warm for him, so he sat and ate his chicken dinner while everyone else was eating pie for dessert.

He laughed at the jokes, answered when the questions were asked, but Chase couldn't get his mind off of Carl Nelson and how he fell from the sky over the forest – and *then* got buried. Who bothered to shove someone out of a shuttle or heli, then went to find the body and bury it afterwards? Most would just leave it as it was and

let the animals take care of it. The burying after part –
that's what didn't fit.

"Are you with us?" Myke asked Chase, her voice pitched
low as she leaned against his shoulder. "Need to talk or
something?"

"Naw, I'm good. Just a strange case and I'm puzzling it
out," Chase replied.

"Let's talk it out over a beer when this is done, yeah? I'm
good with puzzles."

"Maybe. I'll think about it. Thanks for asking, Mykie."
He nudged her and gave her a smile, then looked across
the table at Cassidy. He'd been doing pretty good about
not staring at her all night, but it wasn't easy. She looked
pretty and relaxed and he wanted to see if her skin was
as soft as it looked against that pink silk. But that was not
something he could ever do. Not now, as a co-worker,
and definitely not later as her boss. That was a Halstead
move and he would not bring that kind of shit into his
house.

It was a sacrifice – but it was a sacrifice he was willing
to make for his family.

Chapter Six

Red scrubbed a hand over the brown and gray beard he'd not yet shaved off of his face. His hair was short and dark brown, and tended to stand up straight in the air unless he slicked it down with goop. His eyes were a warm brown and his smile showed white, even teeth, and Lacey thought he was handsome enough to eat with a spoon.

"Come on, Red. If I can go to that FBIS awards banquet thing with you last week, you can do this fundraiser thing with me," Lacey tucked an earring into a hole in her ear and looked at Red in the mirror. "You and Grant talked me into running for mayor, now you're both going to have to deal with the minutiae of it, just like me."

Red had to admit the gown she was wearing did amazing things for her figure – and his libido. "Okay, I need about fifteen minutes to shower, shave, and get dressed." He turned towards the bathroom and Lacey sighed.

"That's so not fair. I've been getting ready for over an hour." She leaned in to kiss his cheek, then smiled. "But I bet you could get me out of this thing in about five minutes. Think about that while we're sitting under the spotlights."

Red pulled her against him and nuzzled her neck. "Woman, you're going to be the death of me with ideas like that. My tux is in the clothes press. Pull it out for me?"

Lacey chuckled and watched him duck into the shower before she went to pull out his tuxedo. Didn't matter what she wore, he was going to look amazing standing beside her. Then again, the deep blue of her silk gown made her blue eyes pop and discreetly clung to healthy curves before spilling around her feet where she wore gold flats to go with the gold cuff wrist device and the twist of gold and sapphires that wrapped around her neck and spilled delicately into her cleavage. Lacey's silver-streaked auburn hair was cut in a short pixie style that needed little fussing, but she'd added some volume and a dusting of gold with the hair product she'd brushed into it. She'd be fifty-six before she took office – if she won – and she couldn't stop the rush of excitement at the potential of a new career.

Grant was hosting the event at the country club housed in Highland Estates, the development of high-end homes where he'd built a home for his mom so she'd be safe. The Estates had their own shuttle landing strip, country club, medical facility, convenience vendors, and wide plots of land that gave each home privacy, space, and views of the surrounding mountain valleys.

Security was tight for the event, making sure only those who had been cleared and bought tickets could get in. Grant tucked Ellery's hand into the crook of his arm and escorted her to the table right in front of the stage. Her gown was black silk studded with crystals so it looked like the night sky full of stars. One shoulder was bared and Elle's long black tresses had been threaded with crystals to mimic the cloth of the gown. He couldn't keep his eyes off of her.

"I'll get us some drinks, then we can relax for a few. Ma's coming with Red in the heli, so she'll be here momentarily," Grant said to Elle. "Wine or something soft?"

Elle gave him a kiss. "Ginger-ale or sparkling water with lemon would be great, thank you."

The venue filled with those who'd managed to pay the entry fee to get a chance to be on a list with the rich and famous. They didn't need to pay to get to talk to Lacey Foster since she'd made sure she was available to people at breakfast meetings, park picnic gatherings, and school functions. In fact, while this was called a 'fundraiser' event, the funds they were raising would go to several charities. Not one cent would touch the election coffers, since Lacey had paid the one million credits, the maximum allowed, from money Grant had invested for her.

A chair scraped and Ellery turned to look, then gasped in surprise. "Mama! Doda! I didn't know you were coming?"

A woman with a shoulder length tumble of auburn curls and bright gray eyes took a seat next to her daughter and leaned in to kiss her cheek. Saoirse Riordan was over fifty, but looked like she could be her daughter's age. Irish pale skin over a farm wife's sturdy figure gave her an ageless appearance. The silvery-gray dress and jacket she wore brought out her eyes and matched the gray accents on her partner's suit. Hawk Adler leaned over to kiss his daughter's cheek then settled in beside Saoirse. His Cherokee heritage showed in the dark hair threaded with gray, dark eyes that glinted with intelligence and amusement, and the tanned skin he shared with his daughter.

"Lacey sent us a couple of tickets and asked us to please be here, but she wouldn't say why," Saoirse told Ellery.

Grant returned with their drinks and smiled at Elle's parents. "Glad you could make it. I asked a server to come by to get your drink orders. There will be a speech or two before we get to eat."

"How's the work on the farm going?" Elle asked them.

"It's going well. We should have the inside of the house finished this week," Saoirse said. "But the outside repairs are going to take some time."

"I'll just be glad to be able to use the whole place soon, and not the two rooms we've been living in while everything was worked on," Hawk added. "I'm also glad they've been working on the barn, too. I want to get some animals settled before the weather turns cold."

"Our place is almost ready for things like flooring and cabinets," Ellery said. "The outside is done and the inside wiring and plumbing is finished enough for the walls to go up. I'm excited to see how it all comes together."

"Elle and my mom have been talking interior design every time they get together," Grant told Hawk.

"Same with Ellery and Saoirse. It's all colors and fabrics and all of that." Hawk gave a soft chuckle. "I just know that they do a good job with making a comfortable, beautiful home. I'll tend the animals and Saoirse will handle the gardens, and we'll both take care of something we never thought we'd call our own again."

"Good people," a voice spoke over the audio system and filled the room. As they turned to the stage, they saw a slender black man with tight braids, dressed in a black suit over a black silk shirt. "I'm Cody Banks, Lacey Foster's aide. I'm here tonight to thank you all for coming and to ask you to please take your seats.

"Servers will be coming around to take drink orders and leave appetizers on the tables. Food will be served after the speeches, and there will be live music and dancing after the meal. Again, thank you all for coming."

The murmurs of voices rose for a few minutes, then settled down as people found their seats and got comfortable. The room held about five hundred people with small round tables set to seat six people at each one. Lacey and Red would sit with them at their table when the speeches were done.

Blue tablecloths, white napkins, and red flower arrangements were tasteful and went well with the cream walls, dark gray carpet, and polished wood trim of the function hall. The stage was set up with three arched windows behind it that reflected the light of the crystal chandeliers against the twilight mountains fading into night.

Grant glanced at his wrist device, then tapped it and got to his feet. "I'm up. Time to introduce my mom."

Cody spotted Grant and went to shake his hand. "Everything's all set. Ms. Foster and Mr. Jefferson are in the alcove and he'll join you at the table after you introduce her. I'll go introduce you now. Ready?"

Grant chuckled. "Cody, breathe. I'm ready. We're all ready. Everything's going like clockwork."

"That's what I'm afraid of," Cody muttered under his breath, then slapped on a bright smile and went up on stage.

"Good people, I'd like to introduce the candidate's son, Grant Davidson Foster. He's also the CEO of Foster Consolidated, a universal logistics and distribution company with global and off-planet locations. Please welcome Grant Foster." Cody stepped back and applauded, then the rest of the room gave a short round of applause before Grant stepped up to the podium.

"Good evening, everyone. The proceeds from this event will go to support a couple of local charities, and one that is dear to my own heart. My mother and I have been active in charitable works for years, and while I was away, mom was very active in our local community. It's with this in mind that I'd like to thank her for agreeing to put half of tonight's proceeds into a new organization. Created to help Lake County farmers and landowners keep their property and avoid being cheated or defrauded, the Adler-Riordan Cooperative will be a resource to help Lake County fight the conglomerates and corporations that threaten to strip our people of their homes and land."

Grant's gaze landed on Ellery, then shifted to where her parents sat, stunned. "My promised partner and Lake County police sergeant, Ellery Adler, watched this happen to her own parents. Seeing how hard they've worked to reclaim their home and their heritage made an impact on me and I wanted to make sure others had the same resources available." He held out a hand. "Hawk Adler and Saoirse Riordan are here tonight, and this is in honor of them."

Grant started to clap and Hawk stood, then helped Saoirse stand. They turned and waved as the room filled with applause, then sat together with Hawk's arm around Saoirse's shoulders.

"Now, I have the honor of introducing my mother, the future mayor of Lake County, Lacey Davidson Foster." Grant said the words, applauded as Lacey came up on the stage, then kissed her cheek before he left the stage and sat back down.

Red came out and slid into a seat with a smile before he turned to watch Lacey on stage.

"Thank you, Grant, and thank you, everyone," Lacey began. Her speech was concise, efficient, and didn't assume she would automatically win, even though she was the only candidate running for the office. They had two days left for someone else to file if they wanted to run, but there had been no rumors or whispers of another candidate.

"And with that, I'd like to thank you all for coming, for donating so generously to the charitable causes outlined in the program, and for supporting me as your candidate for mayor. Enjoy the meal and the music, and come by after the meal to talk." Lacey stepped down from the stage and took her seat beside Red as Cody signaled the servers and the band started to play.

"Excellent job, Mom," Grant said as he lifted his glass in a toast to Lacey.

"Yes, well done," Ellery said as the rest of the table lifted their glasses in a toast.

"I can't believe y'all put our names on something so wonderful," Saoirse said. "I remember how frustrating and futile it all seemed when we were trying to keep them from stealing our home. It changed something in all of us."

Grant slid an arm around Ellery and kissed her temple. "I saw how hard Elle worked and what she was willing to sacrifice to get your home back. We agreed this was something we could do to help others. The files the Halsteads kept were not great, but as we work our way through Jeffrey Morris's documentation, we've found several families that suffered the same way you all did."

A chirp from Elle's wrist device and she was on her feet. "I have to take this. Excuse me." She slipped into the alcove where Lacey had waited to give her speech and answered the call. "Adler here."

"It's Chase. I've been trying to reach you or Grant or Red for the last thirty minutes. Someone blocking signals there or something? I need to talk to Red. We found a second body in Pisgah and it's deep in the National

Forest, so it's now a federal case. I don't trust the ranger assigned to this case, Belfleur, so I want to see who Red can send out for this."

"A second body?" Elle asked. "What do you mean?"

"I was on a call a few days ago where we found the body of Carl Nelson. It's weird. Autopsy said he died from blunt force trauma suffered from a fall of several thousand feet. As in, pushed out of a heli or shuttle," Chase said. "Now we've got another body, Steven Cragan, who looks like it was the same kind of thing."

"Okay, I'll get Red to call you — and I'll ask Grant about the signal blocking. Give me fifteen," Elle said and headed back to the table. She leaned in to Red and murmured in his ear, then sat down next to Grant as Red got to his feet and went to call Chase.

"Someone blocking signals around here?" Elle asked Grant.

"No, not that I know of, why?"

"Chase couldn't get through to any of us for about thirty minutes. Said it was like the signal was being blocked or something."

Grant pulled out his phone and tapped a few times, then frowned. "Something did interfere with the signal earlier, but it appears to have stopped. I'll get someone on it."

The servers came around and placed salads and bread, filled water glasses and so on. As people began to eat, the music suddenly cut out and a man stood at the podium. He looked to be in his mid-thirties with white blonde hair cut short on the sides and a slight wave at the top. His skin was pale and his eyes were an icy blue. He wore a dark blue suit over a white shirt that fit well to his athletic figure as his hands gripped the sides of the podium. "Ladies and gentlemen, forgive my interruption. I know you're all here to support your mayoral candidates, but only one name was on the program."

He leaned back and gave them all a smile. "As of two hours ago, there are now *two* candidates for mayor of Lake County. The lovely Ms. Foster, and myself – Folsom Bentley. There's a data cube being placed on each table so you can download my information and campaign goals. Thank you, and have a great evening."

Lacey got to her feet and met Mr. Bentley as he came off the stage. She offered her hand and gave him a warm smile. "I don't believe we've had the chance to meet, Mr. Bentley. Where do you come from?"

Bentley looked at her hand, then gave it a brief shake before he released her. "From here and there. Don't worry, ma'am. My paperwork is in order. I won't take up any more of your time. Good evening."

When Bentley turned to leave, Ellery briefly got in his way. He bumped into her and she gasped as some of the water in her glass spilled on her gown.

"Oh, no. Can't you watch where you're going? Here, hold onto this for a minute." She handed Bentley her glass and grabbed a napkin to wipe at the damp spot. He shoved the glass back at her and she used the napkin to capture it before he stormed away, never saying a word.

Elle smiled, poured the remaining water into another glass and held the napkin-wrapped one in her lap until she was sure Bentley had left. "I need to go bag this for prints and get it to the lab. That asshole was wearing a Univy pin in his lapel. We need to find out more about him."

"Univy?" Hawk said as he half-rose from his seat. "Pardon my language, but fuck those assholes."

A server reached around Hawk and a data cube was placed on the table. Ellery shook her head and put a finger to her lips. She mouthed to Lacey, "Get these collected and out of here."

Her mother calmed her father down and they all sat silent while Elle helped get the cubes gathered up. Once they were boxed up, Elle put them in her trunk. Grant gave her a kiss and made her promise to be safe before he went back inside and Ellery headed to the station.

Time to get some answers.

Chapter Seven

Red listened to Chase's report and scrubbed a hand over his face. "Okay, I'll send two of my best to run the case with you, and I'll make sure you don't get shoved aside. Tell Belfleur the FBIS is taking it over and he can file his complaints with Senior Special Agent Redmond Jefferson."

"If it's okay with you, I'd like to keep Sergeant Angela Williams in the loop as well," Chase said. "She's with Pinehaven PD and was at the scene of the first body."

"Right, because it was at the spot where the forest, Pinehaven and Lakeridge all come to a point and it could've fallen into any one of those jurisdictions," Red said. "It just happened to be in Lakeridge's the first time – and deeper into the federal lands this time. Yeah, keep her in the loop in case we get any more bodies dropping from the sky."

Chase felt better when Red disconnected the call. At least he'd be able to keep an eye on the case and maybe figure out why two men from northern Virginia were dropped from the sky over western North Carolina. He got up from his desk and headed down towards the lab to see if they'd pulled any more info from Nelson's personal effects. That's when he spotted Ellery in the hallway.

"Hey, Elle, what're you doing here? I thought you were at the event tonight," Chase said as he reached out to take the box out of her hands.

"I was. We had some excitement. Hold it until I can be sure these are deactivated," Elle warned him and opened the lab door. Once inside the lab, she hurried over to the Farraday closet and gestured for him to put the box inside on the floor. An evidence bag was lifted from the top and she shut the door, then sighed. "Okay. Those data cubes were dropped on every table at the event after someone named Folsom Bentley announced he was also running for mayor. I promise you they're sending as well as receiving, so we got them boxed up and I brought them here as fast as possible."

"Woah, okay. And what's that?" Chase asked as he pointed to the evidence bag.

"A water glass that he grabbed. I'm hoping to get a good set of prints off of it."

"Let's see what you've got," Chase said and moved over to the scanner. He watched as Elle put on gloves and pulled the glass from the bag, recording everything as each step was completed. The glass was set on the machine and they stepped back as it went to work.

"Four separate entities prints are on this glass. Missy Brown and Shawn Daley, two persons employed as staff and registered with Events First, a catering company located in Lake County, North Carolina. One set belongs to Sergeant Ellery Adler of the Lakeridge Police Department. One set belongs to Daniel Folsom Bentley, Chief Executive Officer with TechEd, a technology training company." The computer spilled the information, then stopped.

"Give us more information on Bentley and on TechEd," Chase asked.

"TechEd is a wholly owned subsidiary of Univy Universal Corporation with offices in Washington, DC, Fredericksburg, Virginia, Raleigh, North Carolina, and Salt Lake City, Utah. Daniel Folsom Bentley is listed as a resident of both Reston, Virginia and Pinehurst, North Carolina."

"How long as Bentley lived in Pinehurst?" Elle asked.

"A home was purchased in the Longview Estate compound six months ago under the shared names of Daniel Folsom Bentley and Univy Universal Corporation."

"Six months," Chase said with a sigh. "Just enough time to qualify for residency before running for mayor. I'm not buying it. Let's dig in to that and find out when it was really purchased and who lived there before Bentley took up residence."

"Is he going to heli between Pinehurst and Raleigh?" Ellery asked. "What the hell is going on?"

"Maybe he's taking a sabbatical to play at being mayor so Univy can get their hooks deeper into Lake County," Chase said. "That's what I'd do if I were them. We cost them a lot of money and time. Now they want to try a different tactic." He paused and turned to Ellery. "Who's the best analyst you know?"

"Mykal Cutler," Elle said without a moment's hesitation.

"Let's lock this up and I'll go see what Myke is up to," Chase said with a tight smile. "You should go back to the event and keep an eye on things there."

Elle reclaimed the glass then locked it up in evidence while Chase copied the lab file to his wrist device before he escorted Elle back to her car.

"Be safe, little sis. I'll let you know what I learn from Myke," Chase said as he shut her car door. "Good work tonight."

Elle backed the car out of the lot, then caught a glimpse of Chase in the rearview mirror. She was suddenly very glad he was on their side.

Myke sat at the desk in her home office with a frothy latte near to hand that she'd made with her own machine. It was a small luxury she allowed herself, now that she had her own space for such things. She looked up at the monitor she'd hooked up to Red's security system so she could see who was coming and going and help keep those she considered family, safe. She'd even managed to – discreetly – tuck a camera in a tree at her aunt's place so she knew Aunt Caroline was okay.

Myke watched Chase's truck pull up to his place, then watched him go into his home. A few minutes later, he came out in jeans and a t-shirt and walked past Ellery and Grant's to knock on her door.

Curious, Myke got to her feet and went to answer the door. "Chase, what's up?"

He gestured with a container. "Miz Lacey left me a pie. I need to pick your brain, so I figured I'd bribe you with some of the pie."

Chase thought she looked adorable, but he liked his face the way it was, so he didn't tell her that. Her purple and dark brown spikes stood up on the top of her head while the shaved sides and back showed the delicate contours of her skull. Her body was strong and lean with not much in the way of curves – which he knew irritated her to no end. "Like the t-shirt," he said and she laughed. It was dark purple with a fist printed in white, and the words 'bring it' scrawled underneath. The gray cotton shorts and bare feet completed the look that Myke preferred at home - comfortable and functional.

"Come on in," Myke said. "But first, what kind of pie?"

"Mixed berry. Blueberries, blackberries, strawberries all in one. I need to get her recipe," Chase said. "Because I could eat this every day." He put the pie down on the kitchen counter and pulled out two plates. "I'm out of ice cream, otherwise I'd have brought it over."

"I've got vanilla," Myke said. "And you know where the mugs are. Get yourself coffee and I'll dish this up." She got to work while Chase worked the coffee machine before she spoke again. "Okay, so why are you here and what do you need help with?"

"I've got some info and I need a lot more. Elle and I both agree that you're the best analyst we know, so here I am." Chase then filled her in on what had happened and brought up the file on his wrist device before he tapped it to Myke's so the info could transfer over.

"He introduced himself as Folsom Bentley, not Daniel, correct?" Myke asked as she brought up the info on a wall screen.

Chase took a sip of his coffee, then spoke. "Yeah, that's what Ellery said. The lab scan gave us the Daniel part."

"Hmm," Myke murmured as she read over the information.

Chase finished adding the ice cream to the plate of pie and handed it to her. "Let's sit down while your brain works, huh? It's been a long day."

Myke absently took the plate, then blinked and turned to Chase. "Huh? Oh, right. Let's go into my office." She led the way down the short hallway to what could have been a small bedroom, but she'd outfitted into a state-of-the-art working space.

He watched as she put the plate of food down and slid into her chair. Fingers flew over the reflection of a keyboard on the surface of her desk and the clear glass screens that hovered in a semi-circle around her form each showed data streams and images that floated in and out of focus.

Chase settled into a black leather chair and took a bite of his pie. "Myke, eat your pie before the ice cream melts. Folsom Bentley isn't going anywhere in the time it takes to eat."

"He was born to Daniel Bentley and Katya Melnyk, both deceased when Bentley was thirteen," Myke spoke as she filled out a report. "He spent time in the Eaton Park boarding school outside of London, England from age twelve until graduation at age seventeen. After school, he lived with his maternal grandparents, Ivan and Esteva Melnyk in Kyiv, Ukraine until their deaths when he was twenty. He received his first trust fund payment at age twenty-one and settled in Reston, Virginia in a home he purchased outright. School records show an exceptional aptitude for technology and he used that to create TechEd."

"How did his parents – and grandparents – die?" Chase asked.

"Working on that," Myke said. "Looks like his parents died in a car crash, and his grandparents were trapped in their burning home while Bentley was at a party."

"When did Univy buy up TechEd?" Chase finished the last bite of his pie and reached for the coffee.

"About ten years ago, or so it appears. Bentley had done consultant work for Univy from the time he created TechEd, so it may have been a natural progression. He's thirty-seven years old and has been in the top two percent since he was twenty-five."

"He didn't get that rich, that fast, from a tech training company," Chase said flatly. "He was involved in illegals somewhere."

Myke reached for her pie and took a bite. "His first trust fund payout was twelve million credits. Enough to get him the house and get his business started, but not much else. The second payout came when he hit thirty, and it was twenty-five million. The final payout comes when he hits forty and it's another twenty-five million. He's made some good investments, but when he sold out to Univy, they gave him three hundred million credits."

"Three hundred million credits? For a tech training company?" Chase sighed. "Bullshit. I call bullshit."

Myke gave a faint moan at the taste of berry pie and ice cream, closed her eyes, and savored the moment. She swallowed, then took a sip of coffee and washed it down. "They bought his skills and his intellect. They bought a sociopath with advanced tech that they could use."

"How do you know he's a sociopath?" Chase asked. "What else did you find?"

"Two poorly buried police reports that show his parent's car was tampered with. The car's computer was taken over and the car was forced off the cliff and into the ocean," Myke said. "Second was they found traces of accelerant and explosives in his grandparent's farmhouse. I'm betting our boy Folsom was behind them both."

"Un-fucking-believable," Chase whispered. "And he wants to be Lake County's mayor. Well, shit."

"Yeah, my sentiments exactly," Myke replied. "Let's get to work."

Wes wished he could connect with them, he really did. He'd been following the situation as best he could, but when they mentioned Folsom Bentley, he had a memory of a phone call from a man who said he was the director of Univy and that he wanted his best technical person, a man named Folsom Bentley, to look at his Master Key.

Of course, Wes had denied the key even existed because it was a top-secret project for the government – not for Univy. He'd reported the call, then promptly forgot all about it. Now, he wished he could tell them what he knew.

Chapter Eight

The gleaming glass and the view outside of Milos Owens' office was not being appreciated this morning as he paced the room, an earbud in one ear.

"What the hell happened? You said this was foolproof. Not *one* data cube picked up anything?"

On the other end of the call was Folsom Bentley who sat on the patio behind his North Carolina home, a pot of coffee next to him and a pair of beautiful, naked women in the elaborate pool a few feet away.

"What can I say? The transmission blocking seemed to impact the cubes. They're not from my company, so I can't be completely sure what happened. Faulty product," Folsom said as he took a sip of coffee. "It's not that big a deal, Owens. We'll get what we need to discredit the old lady and I'll take the mayoral seat by default."

"This has already cost me more in credits and resources than projected. That house you're in, and your campaign, are fully funded by *me*." Owens nearly spit the words into the air. "Which means, get off your ass and get this done. I need those new facilities cleared and ready for production, and those spurs running cargo out of that backwoods hole in the mountains *yesterday*. Do you hear me?"

"Yes, sir," Folsom said. "I hear you. I'll visit the facilities today and get the paperwork expedited electronically."

"You mean you'll hack the county system and get them cleared? Good. Do it. Let me know when it's done," Owens snapped and disconnected the call. Univy may own DESCO, but those soldiers answered to Samuels. If he didn't get some progress showing soon, he might end up a victim of his own property – and that was *not* how Milos Donald Owens planned to go out.

Cassidy crouched beside the boy and girl who sat in chairs against the wall outside one of the interview spaces. "I brought you some water and crackers. I know you've been sitting here a long time."

Raven and Robert Blackwood were eight and six years old, and had come home from school to find their mother's latest boyfriend standing over her unconscious body with a bloody baseball bat. Raven sat with an arm around Robert, his head on her shoulder as he played with one of her dark braids. Two pairs of dark, solemn eyes met Cassidy's as the accepted the crackers and water.

"Thank you," Raven whispered.

"Is our Mama dead?" Robert asked.

"No, she's at the med center, getting taken care of," Cassidy said. "We'll make sure you get over there to see her, soon. Right now, you two are here so we can find out more about what's been going on. Are you feeling up to talking?"

"Yes, ma'am," Raven said. "We'll both tell you everything. Mama said the police could be good or bad, and that we had to trust our judgement. You have kind eyes, so I trust you."

"Thank you, Raven," Cassidy said, her voice soft. She couldn't tell you why the trust of two little kids meant so much – but it touched her. "Let's go into this room over here, now that it's empty. It's more comfortable and private."

She led them into a comfort room that looked like a living room with upholstered chairs, low tables, and a couple of plants. Both kids sat in the same chair, snuggled together. The air purifier kept it smelling clean, but the faint scent of old coffee still lingered in the room.

Cassidy tapped her wrist device to activate the recording for the room and leaned back. "Could you tell me about your Mama? I know that your father died in a shuttle accident three years ago, and I'm sorry you lost him that way. When did Scooter Gibbons start coming around?"

"He showed up after Christmas. Mama met him at the company party," Raven said.

"We stayed with Auntie Lee," Robert added. "She's not our real aunt, but she's like a real one."

"She lives next door and her grands live in Idaho, so she's our aunt because she loves us," Raven said.

"Leanne Rosen is the one waiting for you in the lobby, correct?"

"Yes ma'am. She's going to take us to see Mama, then we'll go home with her," Raven said.

"Where's Mister Scooter?" Robert asked. "He's not going to take his bat to us, is he?"

"No, Robert, you won't have to see Scooter Gibbons again," Cassidy told the little boy. "He's in prison right now and the judge has already sentenced him based on all of the evidence collected. You're safe. You and your mother are safe."

"He hit us sometimes, but if Mama yelled at him about it, then he'd hit her worse," Raven said.

"He made her cry lots," Robert told Cassidy. "And when she locked the door, he broke it."

Cassidy took a breath to calm herself when all she wanted to do was hug these two babies, and then go kick Scooter Gibbons in the balls – repeatedly. She didn't tell the kids that Scooter was in prison because he had screamed that he was going to kill their mother, Renata Blackwood, then the two children, and anyone that got in his way. When he took a swing at one of her officers with the bloodied bat, they'd used their pulse weapon to drop him to the ground. He spent the whole trip to the station screaming about how he was going to kill the Blackwood family and then go after every cop he could find. Cassidy had been amazed to find out there were no narcotics in his system. He was just that angry.

After the Blackwood kids had been returned to Leanne Rosen, Cassidy went into her office and shut the door. She'd heard from Ms. Rosen how the kids had raced across the lawn towards her place, screaming that their mother was dead – and how she'd come out with her own weapon when she spotted Gibbons lumbering after the two kids with the bloodied bat in his hands. He'd turned and went back into the Blackwood house when he'd spotted her with the weapon and smashed the place up before the cops could answer her call.

At least Raven and Robert had a good advocate in Auntie Lee and didn't have to go into the system while their mother recuperated.

"It's always the domestics with kids that rip me apart, too," Chase said as he stuck his head into her office before she could answer the quick tap on the door. "Sorry to barge in, but I just got to my messages and saw that we're supposed to go to a county meeting tonight. Want to share a ride?"

"Oh, hell, that's tonight?" Cassidy said as she swung her chair around and looked at Chase. "When is it?"

"About an hour. I was going to finish up my paperwork, then hit the drive thru for a burger to hold me over until I get home," Chase replied.

"Okay," Cassidy took a slow breath and ran her hands through her hair. "Give me ten, then I'll be ready. And a burger works for me, too. Thanks for the check-in. I probably would've missed the notice until ten minutes before I had to be there."

"Let me go submit my files and I'll meet you in the back lot," Chase told her with a flicker of a smile, then he shut the door and left her alone.

Cassidy closed her eyes and did a quick breathing exercise to calm her emotions back down after dealing with the Blackwood kids, then shut down her system, grabbed her bag, and headed to the women's locker room. She took a minute to freshen up and touch up her makeup, then went out to the lot and dropped her bag in her trunk just in time to see Chase come out. It was time to pull herself together before he saw just how much he affected her. She met him at his truck and climbed in to the passenger seat as he settled behind the wheel.

Chapter Nine

"Thanks for this," Cassidy said as the buckles slid around her. "I'll spring for the burgers as my thanks."

"You don't have to do that, but sure. Thanks," Chase said. He glanced over at her, then back to the road as he pulled out and headed through town to the burger place. The scent of her filled the cab of his truck and he had to stop himself from breathing it in as if it were the first fresh air he'd breathed after a fire. If he didn't pull himself together, he was going to embarrass himself before they got their burgers and fries.

"Do you know what the meeting is about?" Chase asked.

"It's where we tell them why we want to be chief. Why one of us is the better candidate. Then they vote – and we see who ends up being the boss or the assistant boss by tomorrow afternoon."

"Oh, is *that* all," Chase muttered and shook his head. "I've got nothing prepared."

"Don't worry about it," Cassidy said. "You've got a better chance than me at the position anyway."

"You've pretty much been doing the job for the last few weeks," Chase said. "The other two LT's have barely shown up. I'd say you've got a better shot."

"I've got boobs," Cassidy replied, tone dry. "While you have balls. That puts you at the top of their list."

"I know that's still a factor in some places, but it shouldn't be," Chase grumbled. He pulled into the drive thru and placed their order, then glanced over at Cassidy while they waited to pay. "You can eat a burger, large fries, and a chocolate shake and look that amazing? I'm in awe. I have to work out every day to maintain *my* girlish figure."

Cassidy tried to not laugh, but couldn't hold it in. "You're far from girlish, Lieutenant Payne. Trust me on that." She took the milkshake and bag from him as he passed them over to her. "I work out four days a week. I prefer holo suite running on a beach in Maui. It's calming and rejuvenating."

"How many miles?" Chase asked as he pulled into a parking spot in a corner so they could eat.

"Twelve to fifteen," Cassidy said around a mouthful of fries. "I shoot for fifteen, but if I've been out on the street that day, I settle for twelve. I'm not a masochist."

Chase blinked and gave her a wry smile. "No, of course you're not." He finished his burger and washed it down with the soft drink he'd chosen, then looked over at her once more. "I run five miles every day, then do weight training. I used to be the skinny kid who got beat up every day because I was smart and black."

"I got hassled because I was indigenous. Both of my parents were born within the Qualla Boundary and are Eastern Band Cherokee. My mother was an investigator with the FBIS and my father was a firefighter."

"So, you're a legacy?"

"A legacy what?"

"Civil servant," Chase said and balled up his trash and fed it into the processor in the console. "You ready to get going?"

"Yeah, I'm done except for my shake. I can finish that before we hit city hall."

They were quiet on the short drive back across town to the brick and glass structure that housed the county courts and city hall offices. Chase parked and turned off the truck, then turned to look at Cassidy.

"Whichever one of us gets the chief position, I hope we can be friends as well as co-workers," he said. "And I kinda hope you get chief, if I'm being honest. I'll take it if it's offered, but you'd make a good chief."

"Thank you. I think you'd make a good chief, too," Cassidy said as she slurped up the last of her shake and stuffed the cup into the processor. "And yes, I'd like to stay friends either way."

They shook hands and smiled before Chase turned to get out of the truck, then came around to meet Cassidy so they could walk in together. A united front, no matter what was decided.

A little over two hours later, they were both back in the truck as Chase drove back to the station so Cassidy could get her vehicle. They were both quiet until the truck stopped next to her parked SUV and Chase turned to her. "That was not what I expected."

"It was pretty much what I did expect," Cassidy said with a sigh. "Congratulations, Chief."

Chase reached over and took her hand. "Don't. Don't sell yourself short. I think you said exactly what needed to be said, and I'm not so sure you won't get the chief spot. You were concise and clear and you spoke to local issues and local fears. I don't have that kind of fresh view of things around here, so I could only speak in generalities."

Cassidy liked how his hand felt wound around hers and almost missed hearing what he said. "Maybe a fresh view, combined with a close-up view, is what the department needs. What Lake County needs," she said, then gently tugged her fingers free of his grasp. "We'll see what the decision is tomorrow. For tonight, a glass of wine and a soak in my Doda's hot tub is exactly what I need."

"Be safe going home, Cassidy," Chase said. "I'll see you tomorrow." He watched as she slipped from the truck and got into her own vehicle, then waited until she pulled out of the lot and headed towards home. He turned in the other direction and headed towards his home – even though he would've preferred to follow her.

Chase pulled in to his parking space and shut off the truck, then just sat there. He didn't want to go in to the empty house, and he didn't want to go to the gym and run off his restlessness. If he were being completely honest, he didn't know what he wanted.

Okay, he knew one thing he wanted. Cassidy Redbird. The scent of her lingered in his truck and he could sit there and breathe it in. It held hints of peach and jasmine, and Chase didn't care if it was soap or perfume – it was her scent and he wanted to wrap himself in it.

And he didn't believe he had any right to want to wrap that scent around himself, or to even think about Cassidy Redbird that way. Not after what had happened in Raleigh.

Not after he'd let the last woman he loved get murdered right in front of him. Right in front of him and the child he considered theirs.

Janelle Washington had been with the District Attorney's office in Raleigh for eight years when Chase first crossed her path. Long braids that she kept twisted into a knot at the nape of her slender neck and eyes that flashed fire when she was passionate had caught his attention as she went after a particularly heinous rapist in the courtroom. Legs that looked positively magnificent in her suit skirts kept him from being able to fully focus on the words being spoken back and forth between the lawyer and the witness.

She must've felt his eyes on her because she turned to look at him during the brief recess and gave him a faint smile before she turned back to her table and the system embedded in the glass top. The world of lawyers didn't have briefcases and reams of paper any longer – it was all digitized and encrypted and served up on devices that kept everyone apprised of each and every document.

They went out for drinks that evening, and dinner the next night. Chase had never felt for a woman the things he felt for Janelle. He met her daughter, Janissa, two weeks later and the connection was instant. Within two months he had sublet his condo and was living in the rambling old house with Janelle, Janissa, and Sophia, the woman that was nanny, housekeeper, and family in all the ways that mattered.

When he'd asked her to be his life partner, she'd said yes before he'd even managed to get the words out. The band of rubies he'd slid on her finger had been his grandmother's and she never took it off from that day forward.

Janissa called him Papa Chase, as her memories of her biological father were non-existent. Avery Camden had died from an aggressive form of cancer when Janissa was two. He missed her every day, but at nine years old she was safe at a boarding school in Chapel Hill and spent holidays with her maternal grandparents.

He remembered the day it all blew up as if it had just happened – even though it was coming up on two years past. Orlen Sims had been a big-time drug dealer for The Corporation and a six-month sting had Chase finally arresting him for a slew of charges from drugs to murder. It had been a major coup for his career and his name and face had been plastered across every vid screen and news feed.

A week after he arrested Sims, a strike team had attacked the house in the middle of the night. He'd shoved Janissa and Sophia into a bathroom and had them lock the door, but Janelle refused to hide. She pulled out her pulse weapon and shot one of the attackers, then went after another that tried to break down the bathroom door where her daughter hid. Chase killed the third, but he got to the bathroom too late to save Janelle. The shattered door lay across the threshold and the attacker blew a hole through Janelle as Chase came around the corner. He didn't think about it, he vaporized the man's head, then dropped to Janelle's side. His hands were covered in her blood when he looked up and met Janissa's horrified gaze. Sophia clutched the girl to her chest, but Nissa peered out under one arm and saw the whole thing.

He wasn't safe to be around, so he put Janissa into a private boarding school with excellent security and set Sophia up in her own little house near Nissa's maternal grandparents. The girl had family and safety, he made sure of that. It was the best he could do. He couldn't risk her safety, and he couldn't stop being what he was. A cop.

Chapter Ten

Cassidy looked at the cup of coffee in her hand and made herself take a sip. She hadn't slept much the night before, and from the look of Chase where he sat across the table, he hadn't either. They waited in silence while the judicial board for Lake County determined which one of them would run the law enforcement branch of the county.

"This coffee sucks," Chase muttered as he looked over at her. "Are you sure Haversham didn't make it?"

"Officer Havisham isn't allowed to make coffee any longer," Cassidy said with a soft huff of laughter. "Not after he put half a can of grounds into the machine for one pot of brew. It was like syrup."

Chase made a face of disgust, then gave her a smile. "Whatever they decide, I'll enjoy working with you, Cassidy Redbird."

"Same goes, Chasen Payne," Cassidy said, their voices kept to a near whisper.

"Lieutenants," the head of the judicial board spoke and brought their attention to the five members who stood at the end of the table. "We've reached a decision. Lieutenant Redbird, I'd like to congratulate you on being offered the position of assistant chief of the Lake County Sheriff's department." He then turned to look at Chase and said, "Lieutenant Payne, I'd like to congratulate you on being offered the position of chief of the Lake County Sheriff's department. Congratulations to you both."

Chase and Cassidy stood and accepted handshakes and good wishes from the board before Chase spoke up.

"Excuse me," he said and the three men and two women turned to look at him. "You said that we were being *offered* the position. Which means we have to formally accept or decline, correct?"

"It's a formality, but yes, I suppose you could say that," the man who had made the announcement said.

"Chase, what are you doing?" Cassidy asked. She turned to the board members and smiled. "Then I, Lieutenant Cassidy Redbird, accept the position of assistant chief. Thank you for your consideration."

"Cassidy," Chase sighed. "I was going to give you a chance to take the chief spot."

"Why, don't you want it?" one of the women board members asked Chase.

"I wouldn't have gone through this procedure if I didn't want it – but Cassidy Redbird deserved the position," Chase replied.

"Well, she's officially accepted the assistant spot. Do you want the chief spot, or should we consider other candidates?" the head of the board asked Chase.

Cassidy turned to Chase and arched a brow. "If I have to work with some putz like Bobo Fitch, I'll be very displeased."

One of the board members coughed on a laugh and Chase grinned at her. "Fine. Since you put it that way." He turned to the board and squared his shoulders. "I, Lieutenant Chasen Payne, accept the position of chief. Thank you."

The board members gave them each a new badge and ID, then left them alone in the conference room.

"There's a party at Red's tonight. They planned it no matter what the outcome," Chase told her. "Come with me?"

"Are you asking me on a date? How Halstead of you," Cassidy offered, tone dry.

Chase ran a hand over his face and shook his head. "No, Redbird, it's not a date. It's a work function at a private home. Care to attend?"

Cassidy laughed at the expression on his face and nudged him with her elbow. "Lighten up, Chief. Let's go celebrate."

Chase caught her elbow in his hand as she stepped forward into a stumble, and it brought them face to face. His hands rested on her hips as hers instinctively braced against his shoulders. Unplanned, the embrace felt incredibly intimate.

Beneath the suit jacket she wore, her body was firm and warm. Her eyes had tiny flecks of gold in the dark brown that caught the light as she stared up at him. She smelled of peaches and flowers, and he felt drawn in.

Cassidy felt the pressure of his hands on her hips and the shift of his muscles under her palms - and her mouth went dry. She forgot where they were and stared up at him, her breath catching as sensations spiked through her. Her fingers curled into the lapels of his jacket and she felt the solid strength of him, the sense of protection and safety he radiated like the heat of his body under the fabric of his shirt.

He thought about kissing her, tasting those lush lips and pulling her against him. Slowly, he ran his hands up her sides and felt the silk of her blouse and the tremble of her body. The reality of the situation slammed into him, and Chase stepped back and released her. It took a heartbeat or two before the expression of desire shuttered into blankness on his face.

Cassidy watched him shut down and she felt disappointment. An odd reaction, she mused, when she felt like she'd just avoided being devoured.

"Let's get going," she said and turned for the door.

Chase didn't say a word, just followed her out. He didn't trust his voice – and what could he say anyway? Gee, I'm sorry you're so attractive, but I'm a death sentence? A shake of his head and he made his way out to the parking lot and his truck.

"Meet you at Red's?" he asked her.

"I'll be there," Cassidy replied. She got into her vehicle and let out a breath. Her knees were still trembling. New job, new title, and a new boss that had her all out of sorts. Life sure could get interesting.

"For two people who are now going to be working side by side – literally – y'all are doing a good job of avoiding each other," Ellery said to Cassidy as they sat on the stone patio outside Red's place. The firepit spewed sparks into the late summer twilight and the scents of grilled meat and woodsmoke filled the air.

Cassidy looked into her wine glass, then took a healthy swallow before she spoke. "He almost kissed me, and I really wanted him to."

"He who? *Chase?*" Ellery asked as she turned to stare at Cassidy. When she saw the expression on Cassidy's face, she sighed. "Oh, girlfriend, you've got it bad."

"We can't. We work together. We just can*not* go there. Not if we want to keep the department from being as fucked up as it was under the Halstead's."

Elle leaned back and sipped her wine, her gaze going from Cassidy's tense frustration to Chase's thoughtful look from across the patio where he stood with Red, Grant, and Mykal. "I think you're too worried about what the perception would be. People know – now – that the Halstead clan were a bunch of fucking bastards who spit in the face of anything resembling law and order. And people know that neither you – nor Chase – are like that."

"How do people know?" Cassidy asked as she slumped back in the chair. "We're still cleaning up the mess they left behind and I don't see that much, on the outside, has changed."

"You don't see it?" Ellery asked, eyes wide as she turned in her seat to face Cassidy. "Are you kidding me?" She put her wine glass down and started to count off on her fingers. "No more random harassment stops. No more bribes and payoffs. No more sexual harassment at work - unless you count slugs like Beauregard Fitch."

"Slugs like Bobo Fitch are going to be removed from duty soon enough," Cassidy said. "In fact, that's probably on the top of the new chief's list. We couldn't do anything official about that until we had a chief again."

"People can see the difference, Cassie," Elle said as she put a hand on Cassidy's knee. "You've not been out in it as much as I have, but people are grateful and are expressing their gratitude." She laughed and patted her stomach. "I have had way too many baked gifts as thank yous. I keep putting them in the break room instead of taking them home."

"It's a southern thing, right?" Cassidy said as she took a swallow of wine. "Isn't that how we explain all of the weirdness around here?"

Elle gave a soft snort of laughter. "One of the ways." Music filled the space of the patio and Elle got to her feet. "I'm going to get my future partner and see if he'll dance with me."

"When's the celebration?" Cassidy asked.

"When we finish the house. We want to do it in our own space." Elle turned and walked backwards a few steps. "Get your boss and dance with us."

Cassidy watched as Elle tugged on Grant's arm and pulled him into a clear space to start to dance. She sipped her wine and watched them move in synch. Laughter and affection glowed between them and she felt a rush of jealous appreciation. Cassidy wanted that for herself.

Chase watched her watch Elle and Grant. He put down his beer and walked away from the conversation without saying a word.

It wasn't until his hand was right in front of her face that Cassidy noticed Chase stood beside her chair.

"Would you care to dance?" Chase asked her.

She hesitated a moment, then put her hand in his. "Sure, why not?" Here, in the privacy of Red's patio, she felt safe enough exploring what she could never have. Cassidy felt a rush of heat as their bodies brushed against each other when he pulled her close. The music was slow and sweet and they swayed together, her eyes on his lips. She didn't dare look up. Not yet. Not until she could get some control over her racing heart.

"You keep looking at my lips like that, I'm going to think you want me to put them somewhere," Chase's voice rumbled in his chest but those lips she kept staring at, curled into a sexy smile.

Cassidy's face flushed as she imagined those lips in many more places than just her mouth. "Stop it. I'm trying to avoid embarrassing myself here."

"Kissing you wouldn't embarrass me," Chase said with a grin. "And I doubt it would bother anyone around here if we did kiss."

"Are we going to discuss it? Or just do it?" Cassidy murmured.

The music wrapped around them and Chase's arms wound around Cassidy and pulled her tight against him. One hand curled a finger under her chin and tipped her mouth up to meet his. A gentle brush of his lips over hers once, twice, then her hand curled against the back of his neck and pulled him in. Heat surged and light flashed behind his closed eyelids as Chase felt himself fall. Her taste made him want more. The soft little moan as he angled his head to deepen the kiss told him she wanted more, too.

It took every ounce of willpower to pull back long enough to whisper, "Come home with me."

Cassidy stared into those dark eyes and saw stars. Her lips throbbed in time with her heartbeat as she leaned into his embrace. Then his words registered and she stiffened. "I can't. We can't."

"We can," Chase murmured. "We're consenting adults and we want each other. Let me show you how much I want you, Cassidy."

She pushed against the arm that encircled her waist and took a step away from him. "I can't, *Chief.* We can't. I'm sorry." Cassidy whirled away from him, lips swollen, eyes glistening with unshed tears as she grabbed her purse and hurried towards the parking area and her vehicle.

Chase watched her hurry away and shoved his hands in the pockets of his jeans. He couldn't chase after her, he wouldn't – because she was right. He'd let his dick do his thinking for him and that was the last thing he needed to be doing. Instead, he went over to Ellery and Grant and tapped Elle's shoulder.

"Could you make sure Cassidy's okay? She's out at the parking lot," he said. Elle gave a confused nod and hurried off while Grant ran his hands through his hair and groaned.

"Your timing sucks, brother," Grant said.

"I know. I kissed her, she kissed me, I asked her to come back to my place and she took off," Chase said and reached for another beer.

Grant opened a fresh beer for himself and sat on the stone wall beside Chase. He knew precisely why Cassidy would've taken off, but he asked the question anyway. "Why do you think she did that?"

"Because I'm her boss," Chase said and downed half the beer in a couple of swallows. "And right now? I wish I wasn't. I wish we didn't work in the same field, for fucksake. I haven't felt like this since Ja...uh...for years."

"Since who?" Grant asked. "You know, you never told me what was going on in Raleigh, or what kept you there. Maybe it's time?"

"Myke knows some of it. Ask her," Chase said and got to his feet. "I'm going home. Later, Grant."

Grant watched Chase cross the bridge and head up the road to the village, head bowed and feet dragging. Whatever it was, it was obviously a heavy burden for one man to carry alone. He'd ask Myke about it tomorrow and see what he could learn.

Sometimes you had to help family even when they didn't want the help.

Chapter Eleven

The first week with the new job titles had been a lot of adjustment for everyone. The second week was when the shit started to float to the top.

Chase sat behind the chief's desk and stared at Officer Beauregard Fitch who stood just inside the door and had not bothered to salute his superior officer.

"Fitch, come inside and close the door. And salute before you sit your ass down," Chase growled.

Fitch shut the door behind him and sauntered over to drop into a chair. Then he half-assed a salute and smirked at Chase. "What's up?"

"What's up *Chief*, is what you mean, I believe. Yes?"

"Nope. I said what I meant. Why am I here?"

"You're done. Leave your badge and your weapon on the desk."

"I don't think so," Fitch said as he leaned back in the chair and crossed one ankle over a knee. "You see, my Daddy promised me I'd be promoted once they found a new chief. And now that they have, I'm going to be a Sergeant."

"No, you're not. You're fired," Chase said with a smile. "You see, Bo, we have recordings of you taking bribes to avoid arresting people. Taking bribes of credits, gifts, and sexual favors. We have audio and video to back it all up. You're not just fired, you're under arrest." He waved a hand and two FBIS agents came in and stood on either side of the chair Fitch sat in. "Since some of those recordings are outside of Lake County, it became part of a federal case, so these fine agents are here to take you into custody. Now you can leave your badge and weapon and go quietly, or, and I hope – *really* hope this is the case – you can make a scene and we'll have to stun you into submission and drag you out like the trash you are."

Fitch snarled and planted both feet on the floor, his hands on his knees as he leaned forward. "Boy, you're going to be sorry." He started to stand and the two agents each grabbed an arm and slammed him to the floor. He was cuffed, disarmed, and dragged from the office, screaming the whole way about how he was going to gut Chase and watch him hang by his own intestines.

"At least he's creative," Cassidy muttered as she leaned against the door frame to Chase's office.

"Creative and cooked. Are the other two gone?" Chase asked.

"Yep. They were less creative and more amenable. Angry and defensive, but they didn't make a scene."

"I knew Fitch would be difficult, and I wanted his ire aimed at me, not you," Chase said. As she whirled on him, he held up a hand. "No, not because I don't think you could've handled him, but because it was personal for me." He gave her a tight smile. "No one calls me *boy* and gets away with it. Not anymore."

"Okay, I get it. Just don't manage me, okay?" Cassidy said with a faint smile. "I think we've cleaned out the last of the trash. I'll keep an eye on things, but you've got a meeting at city hall in an hour."

"Right, who's that with again?"

"Folsom Bentley and Lacey Foster. You're supposed to talk to them about crime in Lake County and what your plans are now that you're chief."

Chase grinned. "Oh, this ought to be good. I've wanted to get a few minutes with Bentley since he tried that shit at the fundraiser. Maybe I can get something we can use."

"Don't forget your button. It'll record everything, even if he tries to block the signal," Cassidy said.

"I won't forget. I want him to bury himself."

"I don't think that'll happen, but you'll have fun trying."

"Yes, yes I will," Chase said.

"So, tell us, Chief Payne, what are your plans now that you've had time to settle in?" Bentley asked. They sat at a table in the mayoral suite, the three of them equidistant from each other around the round wooden surface that held a tray of coffee, sandwiches, and cookies.

"Plans? As in what kind of plans?" Chase asked. He didn't wear a uniform like Halstead had done, he wore a shirt and slacks, his badge clipped to his belt and the recording button in the lapel of his suit coat.

"How do you plan on cleaning up Lake County?" Bentley said.

"Well, we fired the last three corrupt cops from Halstead's time in office, and we're hiring more staff to fill those seats, as well as to fill the seats left empty for much too long."

"And then what?" Bentley asked. "I want specifics."

"How specific? We're solving crime, protecting the residents of Lake County, and making sure any corruption left in the county is rooted out and dealt with," Chase said. "In fact, we've been working with the FBIS to deal with crime that's crossed county borders – including two murders in the national forest."

Lacey gave Chase a smile and took a bite of a sandwich, then washed it down with a sip of coffee.

"Murders already? Why didn't you prevent those from happening?" Bentley feigned outrage. "How could you let our citizens be murdered in your first two weeks in office?"

Chase's smile disappeared and he leaned in. "The murders happened before I took office, and they weren't our citizens. Both men were residents of Virginia. Someone shoved them out of a shuttle or heli over the forest and let them fall to their deaths. Now, do you have any more questions?"

Bentley gave Chase a look of supreme disappointment and leaned back in his chair. "I fear that when I'm mayor, I will have to replace the Lake County sheriff's department with a more efficient law enforcement entity. You've done nothing to give me confidence." He got to his feet and tugged on his suit coat. "I'll see myself out."

Once Bentley left the room, Chase rolled his eyes and reached for a sandwich. "Pompous asshole," then he paused and looked at Lacey. "Sorry, Miz Lacey, I didn't mean to cuss in front of you."

"Don't worry about it, Chase. He's a fucking asshole and I'm happy to say it. And if I have my way, he won't be back in this office ever again."

"I hope not. You know his last comment was that he'd replace the whole department with DESCO soldiers. That's the last thing Lake County needs."

"I figured as much," Lacey said and dabbed at the corners of her mouth with a napkin. "Myke has some information for you but you need to go to her to get it. She asked me to let you know she would be at her place the rest of the day."

"Want me to give you a ride home?" Chase asked.

"No, I'm good. My driver is someone Red got for me," Lacey said. "And Grant has me in a reinforced vehicle. They're taking my safety very seriously."

"I'm glad to hear it," Chase said and got to his feet. "We already know Univy won't pull punches, so you need to be smart and safe."

"I know," Lacey said and got up to kiss his cheek. "You be careful, too. You've made some powerful enemies, just by being chief. Don't think you're indestructible."

"I won't," Chase said. "But they've really got their work cut out for them if they think I'll go down easy."

Chapter Twelve

Myke glanced up at the monitor that showed who was at her door and hit the buzzer to let Chase in. "I'm in my office," she called out. "Grab a couple of soft drinks out of the fridge, will ya?"

"Got it," Chase yelled back and got two bottles of cola out of the fridge. He dropped into a chair near Myke and handed her one of the bottles. "Miz Lacey said you've got something for me, so I came here right after the meeting."

"Folsom Bentley's prints were found on a gas can at the scene of his grandparent's burnt house. It was ruled arson and the cops had a solid case against Bentley." Myke said as she opened the soda and took a sip. "Everything looked like he'd go away for it. Then the two investigators and the lead cop on the case all ended up with a bad case of the deads."

"And Bentley wasn't charged in their deaths?"

"Nope. He had a solid alibi. He was on a yacht with about thirty other people when the investigator's car went off a bridge. A woman alibied him for the cop's death. Said he was with her all night, and video footage from her building's security cams put him going into her place around eight at night and leaving around ten the next morning."

"Financials?" Chase asked.

"Two payments of fifty thousand credits went to Lunar Vista Limited, a resort company off planet," Myke said. "Two days after the detective was killed, another hundred thousand credits were deposited into the same account. The memo says it was an investment. I think we both know what kind of investment that was."

"And the case was dropped afterwards?" Chase asked. "Just like that?"

"Just like that. I think the top cop was bribed to let it go, but I haven't been able to get into his financials yet to prove it," Myke said. "Ukrainian records are not as streamlined as ours. They're more compartmentalized and it takes multiple approvals and clearances."

"So, Bentley likely killed his parents, then set up a hit on his grandparents, all before he was twenty-one. He's a psychopath, and from my short interactions with him, a malignant narcissist, with delusions of grandeur," Chase said. "Lovely. Just what we want in a mayor." He sighed and took a sip of his soda. "I need something solid,

Myke. I need a way to shut this asshole down before he, and Univy, get their hooks into our county."

Myke glanced at her screens, then turned her chair to face Chase and pulled one knee up to wrap an arm around it, the heel hooked on the seat. "I have a question for you. Have you used that drone yet?"

"I played around with it," Chase said. "Got used to the controls, but no, I've not done any scouting with it."

"Let's take a drive and see what we can see. Bentley's got decent tech security, but I'm better than he is and I found a few threads that I'd like to tug on."

"What do you mean?"

"I found a message from Jonas Samuels to Bentley, something about a lab and spur being built. I think it's on the border of Pinehaven and the national forest, but I can't be sure."

"Samuels. Why does that name sound familiar?" Chase asked.

"He's on the board of Univy, and he was the head of DESCO," Myke replied.

"And he's messaging with Bentley," Chase grumbled. "Yeah, let's take a drive and see what we can see."

They parked on an old logging trail about a mile from the public lot for a popular hiking trail into the forest.

Chase climbed into the back of his truck and uncovered the drone.

"Ever flown one of these before?" he asked Myke.

"Yeah, several times," Myke said. "Why, want me to take it up first?"

"Sure, since you've got the experience. I'll set up the recorder and power it off of the truck so we have plenty of juice," Chase replied. "Let's get her up high enough that we can see what we need to see, but too high for the average person to notice, shall we?"

They sat in the back of the truck and watched the drone rise up above the trees, then Chase tapped his tablet and watched the video as it recorded the flight. Myke kept her eyes on the control tablet and once it was out of visual range, she started a grid scan. "I'm going to follow the road for a bit and see if anything pops."

They were silent and watching for a good half hour before Chase spotted something. "Hold. Go east a little bit. There, see that glint of silver in the trees?"

The drone image shifted closer to the spot Chase pointed out. "Zoom in a little?"

The image grew larger and they both cheered. "We found it!" Myke crowed. "Damn, we're good."

"Yeah, but what did we find?" Chase asked. "It looks like a pretty small building for a lab setup."

Myke brought the image up and enlarged it as the drone hovered. "There's a lot of displaced soil around there. And there's a maglev spur a couple hundred yards away with a building at the end of it. I'm guessing that's a shelter for the train so they can load no matter the weather, and the other building is an access point."

"But the rest of it is underground," Chase breathed. "That's fucking brilliant, but also really stupid. Easy to take a place that's only got two entry points."

"We're not going to be taking it yet, Chase. And it's an FBIS case, so take a breath, okay?" Myke reminded him. "Let's get a good grid scan of the area and make sure we have all of the information possible for Red."

"He's going to want full spectrum, so we'll have to come back at night," Chase said. "You up for that?"

"Gee, golly, are we gonna have a picnic?" Myke teased as she flew the drone in a collection pattern.

"We can, but I'm cooking. I've had your idea of cooking, Mykal Carter and it's nothing I plan on putting in my stomach," Chase retorted.

"Careful, Chasen. I know where you live," Myke said and they both laughed.

Later that evening, when they showed Red the imagery, he hugged them both and kissed their cheeks. "This is fantastic. Good work, both of you."

"It was mostly Myke's work," Chase said. "I just drove the truck and did the recording."

"Her brilliance never fails to impress me," Red replied. "Speaking of brilliance, I hear Bentley is threatening to replace the department with DESCO soldiers?"

"I said that was my suspicion," Chase said. "A suspicion that was confirmed when Myke told me he's been messaging with Jonas Samuels."

"I've got a retired agent as Lacey's driver right now. Andrew Peters. He's only been out a little over a year, and was bored," Red said. "I trust him with her, so that should be good enough for y'all."

"We know how much you treasure Miz Lacey," Chase said. "And she said Grant got her a reinforced vehicle?"

"And two bodyguards, but she doesn't know about those," Red said. "There have been...threats."

Chase glowered and leaned in. "What do you mean, threats? What kinds of threats? How come you didn't report them?"

"I didn't want to get Lacey upset," Red said. "And I was going to tell you, but it's been a crazy couple of weeks." He got up and paced the length of the room a couple of times, thinking about his approach, before he rejoined them and sat back down. "They were messages I intercepted. I've been scanning all of her messages and mail through Andrew and with Myke's help. Since Bentley showed up, there have been a handful of messages with comments that a woman's place is in the home, or old women have no place in politics."

"I'd love to hear them say that to our President," Myke muttered. "She's only a year younger than Miz Lacey and she's on her second term."

"President Elizabeth McKenzie is one of the most brilliant legal and political minds I've had the pleasure of conversing with. She's had a tough agenda, but she's managed to keep us on track," Red said. "But as you both know, there are still pockets of resistance to women holding any power or individual control. The Initiative has been in the forefront of the 'return the patriarchy' movement and they're particularly entrenched in some of the more rural communities."

"They're crazy people with conspiracy theories," Chase said. "But those crazies often get enough of a following to make life...interesting."

"Run into them before?" Red asked.

"Yeah, a few times," Chase sighed and rubbed his hands over his bald head before he leaned back and stretched his arms out along the back of the couch. "Some of them are deceptively normal in appearance – until they're not. Be careful with them. Had one pull a knife on me once with zero warning. He ended up bleeding more than I did, but it was a close thing."

Red shook his head. "If I could get Lacey to wear body armor, I would. I know the stuff we have now is a lot lighter and more flexible than the old stuff, but she still doesn't like it."

Chase grinned. "That gives me an idea. I'll run it by Grant because it's out of my budget, but I heard about this prototype stuff that is being used as a liner in jackets and coats. It's light, flows like fabric, but reacts to pulses, blows, and stabbings as if it were solid."

"I wouldn't mind some of that," Myke said. "If he can get ahold of it, let me know."

"If he can get ahold of it, I'll be asking him for a donation to the sheriff's department, too," Chase told Myke. "We're up against some of the big guys now, and we all need to keep our eyes on a three-sixty swivel. Got me?"

"You're not wrong," Red said. "Not even a little bit."

Chapter Thirteen

Cassidy slowed her steps and let the sounds of the beach wash over her. The holo-suite program was almost as good as being on Maui. The scents and the sounds, the feel of the sand under her feet, it was all very convincing. What wasn't convincing was the chirp of her wrist device, telling her she had ten minutes left in the program.

"Someday, when I'm rich, I'll have my own holo-suite," Cassidy muttered as she walked her cool down. She stepped out of the suite and reset the panel, then slid the handle of her bag over her shoulder and made her way out of the public facility to her vehicle. It was late and a breeze had picked up, the scent of rain on the wind.

Her car unlocked automatically as she approached, so she tossed the bag in the back, then slid into the driver's seat and locked the doors. A bottle of water waited in the console, so she took a few swallows after she started it up, then backed out of the spot and headed towards home.

Her thoughts went to Chase and the kiss they'd shared. She'd had a few good kisses, and a few men that she had had no qualms about going home with, but Chase was different. That kiss? It had been very different for her. Of course, it was the first kiss she'd had in a few years. The last man she'd kissed had been her fiancé back in Nashville, and no matter what she might want to tell herself – Everett Lansing did not even compare to Chasen Payne in the kissing department.

Everett didn't compare to Chase in *any* department as far as Cassidy was concerned. Often, she wondered what the hell she'd been thinking to agree to partner with Everett in the first place. Oh, sure, he'd been handsome enough and he'd been supportive at first. He had plenty of money and took her out to the ballet and opera, bought her jewelry and clothes. He liked the idea of having a woman he could show off, and that all played well in the beginning. But then he started to criticize her clothes, her career – got angry if she was working a case and missed a dinner date or was late getting home. When he spent time at her place, he moved her things around and told her that some of her family treasures were ugly or insulting to him, a white man. She'd gone along with a lot of it because it had happened in tiny increments – like water dripped on stone.

The friends she'd made outside of work began to fade away. Everett thought Maria was crude and insulting. He decided he didn't like the way Ozzie had hugged her when they greeted each other. When Cassidy told him she'd planned a girl's night at her place with Sarah and Jane, he told her to cancel because he had been given tickets to the ballet for that night.

She'd had two inches of her hair trimmed. The length brushed to about mid-thigh, and she kept it braided up into a bun for work, or pulled up with glittering combs and pins when they went out. Everett loved to wrap his hands in her hair, but when she'd had it trimmed, he'd raged, then burst into tears. "A woman's hair is her glory," he quoted from the Christian bible. She didn't get it trimmed for two years.

When her father had taken ill, she'd submitted a leave of absence and prepared to head home to take care of him. That's when it all blew up. Everett had insisted she simply hire a caretaker and stay in Nashville with him. If she wanted to quit her job, he was fine with that – she could take care of his home and move in with him. As long as she left her weapon at work. He didn't want weapons in his home.

He didn't understand family. He didn't understand responsibility, and he clearly didn't understand Cassidy. She quit the Nashville PD, packed up her things, and moved home to be with her father.

She left the four-carat diamond ring in the middle of Everett's bed and drove away. On the way home, she'd stopped at a salon along the side of the road and cut off her hair to just above her shoulders. It was a week later when she went in and had it properly cut to chin length by her cousin Solara who did hair for many of the women of the Eastern Band.

It had chilled her, deep in her bones, how much she had let Everett change who she was and how she lived her life. The idea that she might've gone on to live a life controlled by a man terrified her.

As much as she had enjoyed Chase's kiss, she would never let a man tell her what to do or how to live her life – ever again.

Chase whipped the egg whites and sugar into stiff peaks, then spread it over the lemon custard in each of the eight ramekins. He pulled the meringue into delicate peaks, then put the pan into the oven. A crumb crust, lemon custard, then the meringue topping filled each ramekin before they were set into a larger pan with water that rose partway up the ceramic cups. It only had to bake long enough to lightly brown the meringue, then he'd take them out and let them cool.

When Chase was stressed, or puzzling out a case, he got into the kitchen. Lemon meringue was a comfort food for him, as much as rice and beans with ham chunks or a really good grilled cheese sandwich on crusty bread.

The team had been having twice a week dinners at Red's place to discuss what they were learning about the goings on in Lake County and what Univy was up to. Tomorrow's dinner would have his individual lemon meringue pie cups for dessert - and probably a couple loaves of his rosemary bread. He wasn't going to be heading in to sleep any time soon.

He couldn't get the taste of Cassidy's mouth to leave him alone – or the way she'd felt, pressed against him. He'd seen the brief moment of surrender flicker across her face then disappear when he'd come to his senses and pulled back.

Why had he pulled back? She'd looked lost, then angry or insulted – it was hard to tell which. Either one would work to keep her out of his arms. He only brought death to the people he loved.

He'd looked on Alex Layton as a substitute father, and he was dead. His father was good and loving, but Lemar Payne had been as devoted to the force as he found himself being now. Back then they'd had State police, but during one of the government restructurings, state forces had been divided up into a division of the FBIS or parceled out into the county departments. When the restructuring happened, Lemar took a slightly early retirement package and moved his wife to Florida. His body had been beaten up on the job and the warmer climes meant he didn't hurt quite so much.

Serena Kincaid had been his girlfriend when he was at Duke. Serena with her long auburn hair and olive skin, hazel eyes and a tongue as sharp as a sword – and as gifted. She'd been in the journalism program and they'd met at a party off campus. The best thing he could say about that relationship is that it was like fire and ice. They burned up the sheets, and argued like gladiators. He loved her intelligence and her wit, and her body that did things he didn't know were even possible.

He graduated a year ahead of her and was in the police academy when she'd gone missing. They were supposed to meet to study, have pizza, and share the bed in her tiny apartment. He got there and it looked like there had been a fight. They investigated the hell out of him, but the blood they'd found in the apartment wasn't his.

Two years later, he'd been one of the team that had taken down Jedediah Malone, a serial killer who had raped and murdered twenty-three college co-eds - including Serena Kincaid.

There had been women, now and then, but no one serious until Janelle. Then there was Wes – a man he considered a brother – a reclusive and antisocial brother, but a brother – and someone had murdered him.

People that he got close to? They died. It was just better if he stayed casual friends and avoided entanglements. It was better for everyone, because he was heartily tired of attending funerals.

Chapter Fourteen

The phone was ringing and Chase had to pull himself out of the fog of sleep before he could remember where it was. He'd dropped into bed just before dawn, and it was a Saturday, so he was supposed to be off duty until Monday morning. The only reason someone would be calling him is if there was an emergency no one else could handle.

"H'lo?" Chase grumbled into the phone.

"Papa Chase, it's me, Nissa. Did I wake you? I'm sorry. I'm at Mimi and Gramps' place for the long weekend, so I could call you and talk. They don't let us use the phone unless it's an emergency or scheduling pickups at the Academy, you know. So, I can't just call you and talk. I miss you. How are you doing? Did you get the chief job? Do you have a room I can stay in when I come visit? Could you turn on the vid so I can see you?"

Chase couldn't help the smile that curled his lips when he heard the bubbly voice in his ear. "Hang on a minute, Nugget," he told her and adjusted the pillows so he was sitting up. At least he'd managed to pull on a t-shirt with his shorts before bed, so he was presentable.

He hit the video button and smiled as her face filled the screen. A pang hit his heart when he saw, once again, just how much she looked like her mother. "There's my girl. How are you, Janissa?"

"I'm good, Papa. You look tired, though."

"I was up late, baking. A bunch of us are meeting at Mr. Red's place for dinner tonight. I made my lemon meringue cups."

"One of my favorites," Nissa said and sighed. "I miss you, Papa. When can I come visit and see your new place? And meet your friends from when you were a kid?"

"We'll see how things are when you've got your next break. That's around October, right? It's beautiful here in the mountains then, with all of the leaves changing. And yes, there's a room in my new place that will be yours – as soon as I unpack the boxes I've got stacked in it."

Nissa laughed and rested her chin in her hand. "I know you, you've been too busy to do anything with your place. Did you get the chief job?"

"Yes, I did. Just the other day, in fact. And Cassidy Redbird is my assistant chief."

"Cassidy? You like her?" Nissa leaned in and grinned at him. "Is she smart?"

Chase made a soft sound of amusement. "Look at you, my little schemer. Yes, she's smart, beautiful, and I'm her boss. I can't think of her as anything else."

"Yeah, but you do, Papa. Your face told me." Nissa looked down and bit her lower lip, then looked up again and met his gaze. "You know it's been over three years now. You should find someone to make you happy, and give me brothers and sisters before I'm in college."

"We'll see, Janissa. Now, tell me about your grandparents and your school and how everything is in your life," Chase said.

He listened to the trials and joys of a well-adjusted thirteen-year-old girl who knew she was loved beyond measure, then let her go when her grandmother called her down for breakfast. Chase considered sliding back under the covers, but there was a happy warmth in his chest where Nissa glowed, so he got up, showered, and made some coffee. He had neglected his place and it was time he stepped up and made it a home – before Janissa showed up on his doorstep.

First up was unpacking the few boxes that had been stored in the second bedroom. A couple of them he opened up, then closed again and moved to the top shelf of his bedroom closet. Bits and pieces of his childhood that his parents had given him at some point or another that he simply moved from place to place because he couldn't throw them out.

He found the boxes of books and cookbooks, and spent an hour sorting them between the main living space bookshelves and the shelves up over the island that divided the main space from the kitchen. Another box held a few pieces of art he'd collected or been gifted. The tribal mask his parents had brought back from a visit to Senegal, the woven hanging his father's sister had made when Chase had been born – they found places on the walls alongside a watercolor he'd bought from a street vendor, and some framed photos of scenery. He didn't put out photos of people – those he kept stored on a personal, encrypted cloud device, locked in a safe.

Having photos of the people you loved when you did the job he had done for years? That made them targets. Chase knew more than one cop who had lost family and friends to people they were putting behind bars because they'd seen the photos. He wouldn't take that chance. Granted, they'd found Janelle because of her job with the DA's office, but it could as easily been because he'd arrested Orlen Sims, not because she'd prosecuted him.

The only portrait he hung up was in Janissa's room. A line drawing of Chase and Janelle that had been done by a friend of theirs. He had his arms around her and her head was tipped to tuck under his chin. She looked at the artist while he looked into the distance. Janissa loved the print and he'd given her a copy of it, but he'd hang the original here, in her space. In his house.

Myke's voice called out from beyond the French doors off of the main room. "Chase, are you alive in there?"

"Yeah, Myke. Just taking care of some things. What's up?" he called back as he made his way to the open doors.

Myke stepped into the screen porch and took a look through the open doors into the living space. "Finally moving in all the way, huh? Good for you. It's important to make a place into a home when you plan on staying for a while."

She moved past him to look at the books in the shelves and the little things he'd started to put around. "What made you finally decide to unpack? Getting the job?"

"No, my daughter called and demanded I make sure there was a room ready for her when she visited."

"Daughter?" Myke asked and turned to look at him in surprise. "I didn't know you had one."

"She's not mine by blood, but I helped raise her from the time she was five," Chase said. "Her mother was murdered three years ago, so now she goes to a boarding school and stays with her grandparents on school breaks."

"Tell me about her?" Myke asked as she leaned against the arm of a chair.

"I'm not used to talking about her," Chase said with a wry smile. "I keep her safe by keeping her separate. Her name's Janissa and she's thirteen now. Smart as a whip and looks just like her mama."

Myke remembered something and her eyes gleamed with understanding. "Her mother was Janelle Washington, right? The DA that put Orlen Sims away? I read about that case and that you'd arrested him. I didn't know there was a kid."

"We kept her out of it as much as possible, but Jan was murdered right in front of her just before she turned ten," Chase said and the pain seared through him all over again.

Myke saw it on his face and silently went to give him a hug. "I'm sorry, Chase. So sorry." She held him for a moment and he put his arms around her and let the pain fade once more.

"So, teenage girl gets a room in Dad's place, and..."

"Papa. She calls me papa. And yeah, I have no idea how to decorate a room for her. I figured a bed, a dresser, nightstand, and desk with a chair."

"And Papa Chase needs help. I was a teenage girl once. What's her favorite color?" Myke asked.

"You were a teenage girl? Really?" Chase teased, then took the half-hearted swat Myke aimed at his arm. "She likes all colors. Bright and bold."

"You order the furniture, I'll get the bedding and curtains and a few things to make it more comfortable for her until she's here and can pick out stuff for herself. Sound like a plan?"

"Sounds like a plan," Chase said. "Thanks, Mykie. She's really into her African and Scottish heritage right now, so maybe you can find something Celtic or tribal that she'll like?"

"I know just the thing. Oh, I came by because I got some more info on the lab photos. FBIS put a satellite on it and we've got ground penetrating imagery. Come on over and check it out."

Chase left the last box open on the coffee table and locked up his place before he joined Myke outside.

Neither one of them saw the drone high above the village, recording their interactions and conversation.

Chapter Fifteen

Folsom Bentley enjoyed the finer things in life. The Waterford crystal glass that held his bourbon, the silk lounging pants he wore on his body, and the exquisite woman he had tied and gagged in his playroom.

He took a sip of his drink as he stepped through the doorway, then closed the door behind him and put the glass to the side. His muscular torso and arms were bare, as were his feet. All he wore were the pristine white silk pants with a drawstring tie.

For him, this was a holy place and he was dressed for a ritual.

The room was windowless, soundproofed, and deco-rated in the latest equipment for the discerning sexual sadist. The suspension rig, for example, was of titanium with the cuffs extending from the floor and ceiling at the whisper of a command. They were currently holding the delicate wrists and ankles of a woman he'd had shipped in from Martinique. When you had the kinds of connections he had, you could, literally, get anything.

He didn't know her name. He didn't care. He knew she was barely legal and was, until him, untouched sexually. Exactly as he'd ordered.

She whimpered as he brushed a finger down her cheek, too terrified to turn her head away. Silky black tresses brushed mid-back and wide, dark eyes struggled to focus, the pupils blown wide open as the drugs worked their way through her system. He liked them responsive, but not combative, so he'd had a cocktail designed that gave them the energy of a companion robot and the ability to feel, and fear, everything he would do to them.

The terror was delicious, he had to admit. It was one of his favorite flavors.

"Now, my lovely, shall we get started?" he said to the girl, then reached for his tray of tools.

The recording captured every sob and scream, until the screaming stopped.

Red knocked on the door frame of Chase's office before he stepped inside – and shut the door behind him.

"Uncle Red, what brings you down? Are you okay?" Chase asked as he got to his feet.

"I'm fine, Chief," Red said with a tired smile. "I could use a coffee, though. Came in from DC a couple of hours ago and I haven't been home yet."

Chase went over to the coffee bar in his office and got a cup brewing for Red. He pulled out a cup of fruit and handed it to Red with a fork. "Here, eat this while the coffee is brewing. It'll give you an energy boost. So, what's got you sitting in my office? Not that I mind you dropping in for a visit, but I'm pretty sure that's not what this is."

"We got the tracking info for flights over Pisgah for the few days around the time frame the coroner gave for the time of death on those two men," Red said as he accepted the fruit and the fork. "I wanted you to know from my lips that we have a suspect and we can't act on anything right now."

Chase pulled the mug of coffee from the machine and set it on the low table between two chairs, then sat in the other chair across from Red. "Who is it?"

"The only shuttle that was in the air over Pisgah during those two days that encompass the ten-hour window of time of death, belongs to Milos Owens."

Chase dropped back in the chair and scrubbed his hands over his face. "Because we have no evidence proving

Owens pushed those two men to their deaths, we can't even shake him down to try and get him to slip up, because he's intimidated half of the politicians in DC. Right?"

"Pretty much hit the nail on the head," Red said as he finished up the fruit and reached for the coffee. "However, we can add this to the list of things to pile on him when we finally do get a solid case. You know these things take time, Chase. We're in the early days, yet."

"I know," Chase said with a grumble in his voice. "And I appreciate you telling me in person. Next time, you can just ask me to swing by on the way home, y'know. You have more than earned that kind of courtesy."

"That's not the only information I have to share," Red said as he took another swallow of coffee. "We're building a case against Folsom Bentley, but I have to step back because of my relationship with Lacey Foster."

"What kind of case?" Chase leaned forward now, elbows on his knees. "Because that fucker sets off every red flag I've got whenever he's near."

"As you know, Myke's been looking into him. Hard core. She got enough together to get the FBIS to open a case with Interpol in the deaths of his parents and grandparents."

"You mean reopen the cases?"

"No, I mean open a case. There was never a case filed on his parents' deaths, and the excuses for cops that worked his grandparent's case are both dead and the file is missing."

"Fucking unreal," Chase muttered. "Money can do that so easily. So, is that the case or is there more?"

"Myke has found a pattern that may or may not lead back to him. She's working on it, but there's not enough yet. Seems that there have been bodies of young women that turn up whenever Bentley spends more than a week somewhere." Red finished the coffee and put the cup down. "They're all young, beautiful, and the cause of death is from some kind of drug cocktail no one has ever seen before. Their bodies are sterilized as if they were going into surgery, so no DNA or fibers are available." He paused and cleared his throat. "And they all have the same kind of genital mutilation."

"By the stars," Chase whispered. "He's a fucking monster. We need to make sure he's never able to hold office anywhere."

"I'm only telling you this because I need you to keep an eye out for any bodies that drop – and if it is Bentley doing this, as we suspect - they will drop. We need you to call the FBIS the minute you find something that might fit the information I've given you. Just...don't make it public yet. We don't know if there are any still lurking with divided loyalties."

"Overt loyalties? Yeah, we've found them. But I hear you, Red. I know there are probably a few that still pine after the Halstead days. I'll keep it between myself, Cassidy, and Ellery. If something pops, I'll let you know."

"Thanks, Chase," Red said as he got to his feet. "Be safe out there, son. You're too important to us." He paused and put a hand on the younger man's shoulder. "Too important to me."

"You stay safe, too, Red. You're important to me as well," Chase said and stood to give the older man a half-hug.

He watched as Red slowly made his way out of the office and down the hall before he went next door to Cassidy's office and tapped on the frame of the open door. It was time to update his second in command, no matter how much he'd rather avoid being alone with her.

"Got a minute?" Chase asked as he stuck his head into her office.

"Sure, let me just finish this report," Cassidy said as her fingers flew over the reflection of a keyboard on her desk.

Chase stepped in and closed the door behind him, then leaned against it while she finished up her work. He had to admit, she looked good. Really good. The dark gold jacket she wore over an emerald green silk top looked classy and professional. He knew she was wearing navy blue slacks that fit to her backside in such a way he'd had a hard time not staring. Okay, not staring much.

"Okay, I'm done," Cassidy said, then looked up to see Chase still stood by the door. "Well, come sit down. You don't need to stand all the way over there."

"Red was just here and gave me some information that I need to share with you – and that we can tell Ellery, but that's it. Until we're completely sure we have a team that has our backs, we can't let the information get out."

"Now you've got me worried," Cassidy said as she slid her computer screen to the side. "Talk to me."

Chase sat down and filled her in on everything Red said, and then told her what he and Myke had discovered about the lab. When he was done, he sat back and watched her face as she processed the information.

"Basically, what you're telling me, is that we've got a lot of probable cause but not enough information to act on – yet – because the man has connections and a ton of credits."

"That's it in a nutshell, yeah," Chase said. "We keep an eye out for bodies, we keep an eye on Bentley, and we wait to see what they do with the lab now that it's nearly completed. The scans showed that the air filtration system was finished a few days ago, and that's the last piece before they start production. It's already furnished and they've even got an underground parking facility so we can't get a look at how many vehicles are there unless we do more scans."

"We can put surveillance up in the trees around it, though," Cassidy said. "You just told me there's only two ways in or out – and one is the road into the garage and the other is a back door that comes out near some rocks and has no footpath or anything around it."

"They probably have their own equipment up," Chase said.

"Or they don't have it up yet. Either way, we can go in at night in full camouflage and set them up ourselves."

"You're going to climb trees to put equipment up?" Chase asked her with a laugh.

"I can. Or we can use the technology we've been given by the FBIS when we had to put equipment up around the Halstead operations." She really didn't like that he'd laughed at her, but she kept her expression serene.

"The department still has all of that?" Chase asked.

"It does. Or, I do. I kept it in my gear locker until recently. Now it's in that cabinet over there," Cassidy said as she pointed to a black metal cabinet in the corner. "Are you capable of driving in the dark or should I handle this alone?"

Chase had the good sense to wince. "I'm sorry, I didn't mean to be insulting. I know you're capable of climbing trees, but it isn't the smartest tactic when dealing with a facility like this."

"Smart man, walking that back," Cassidy said with a tight smile. "Let's go do it tonight, unless you have other plans?"

"I don't, and yeah, tonight is good. The sooner we get it done, the sooner we can start building a case. Do you have night gear here or do you want me to pick you up at your father's place?"

"I've got the gear here," Cassidy said.

"Good, then tell everyone we're going to dinner together and bring the gear up to my place in the village. We can change there and borrow Red's Range Rover. It's black and will handle the terrain better than either of our vehicles – and be easier to hide."

Cassidy opened her mouth to complain about him bull-dozing her, but closed it when she realized he had a good plan. "Okay, I'll be at your place a little after six."

"Don't be late, Assistant Chief. I'd hate to leave without you," Chase teased.

"You can't leave without me. I have the equipment," Cassidy fired back.

Chase just smiled at her as he stepped out of her office and went into his own. Tonight was going to be fun. He just knew it.

Wes enjoyed watching the growing romance between Chase and the lovely Cassidy, but he desperately wanted to smack Chase in the back of the head for thinking he wasn't worthy. Okay, so worthy wasn't the right word – maybe he didn't think he was safe enough? To Wes's eyes, Cassidy seemed like a woman who could take care of herself and anyone else she wanted to protect. Chase needed someone like her to balance him out and remind him that life was more than being a knight or guardian for everyone in the universe.

In chess, a knight was the only piece that could jump over other pieces. It captured enemy pieces by landing on them and was most effective when it occupied the center of the board, as that's where the most possible moves could be found.

The knight was also the most vulnerable when it was in the center of the board, and was vulnerable to traps.

Wes hoped Chase knew to watch his back.

Chapter Sixteen

Chase had all of his gear on except for the hood and mask when Cassidy arrived at his place. She handed him a heavy case then went into his bathroom to change into her gear.

"Open that up and take a look at what we're working with before we get on the road. I saw the Range Rover outside – Red's fine with us using it?" Cassidy asked as she left the door open a crack while she changed.

"Yeah, he even sent a few more devices to post along the main road so we can triangulate what drives past with what pulls in," Chase said. "There's also an identification reader we can put on the road and it's legal to post it there."

"You up for this?" Cassidy asked him. "I'm not being snarky, I'm serious. You look tired."

"I'm up for it. Yeah, I'm tired, but not dangerously so," Chase closed the case and leaned back to look up at her. "This job takes a lot more than I expected. I'm not complaining, but it's an adjustment."

"There's a reason you have a second in command, Chief," Cassidy told him with a smile. "You don't have to do it all on your own. We're a team, remember?"

Chase stood and handed her one of the equipment cases. "I'm working on that. I haven't had a working partner in about three years, so I got used to just handling it on my own." He paused, then continued. "I'm probably going to need you to remind me now and then."

Cassidy took the case and headed for the door, her clothing bag in her other hand. "I'll try to not be a pest about it," she told him. "But don't get grumpy with me when I do remind you. Agreed?"

"I don't get grumpy," Chase retorted. "But if you *think* I'm grumpy, hand me a bottle of water. I can hyperfocus with the best of them."

"Right," Cassidy said as she dropped her bag in her car, then the gear case into the Range Rover. "I'll stock up on a case of water." She couldn't keep the smirk from her face and Chase caught it as she slid into the passenger's seat.

"Wow, this is a nice ride," she said as she buckled in. "Is this an FBIS vehicle or Red's personal one?"

"Uh huh. Smartass," he chuckled as he got in and started up the vehicle. "It's his personal one. This thing has more buttons than a shirt factory." Chase fell silent and waited until they were on the highway towards Pine-haven before he spoke again.

"I worked out an approach with Myke, using the satellite imagery she'd pulled down. If you pull up the file 'party planning' on your dash screen, you'll be able to see what we worked out."

"You should've included me," Cassidy said, her voice tight. She wasn't going to let him shut her out of anything related to her job. This was a position she'd earned, dammit. Her anger simmered until he spoke again.

"I didn't have time. Myke brought over the updated satellite imagery when I got home and we went over it quick and I uploaded it so you could go over it on the way. If you see any obvious holes or issues, let's figure them out now."

Instead of speaking, and giving herself away, Cassidy took a breath and opened the file. She had to stop knee-jerk reacting to Chase just being Chase – and his being the chief. If he really thought her inept, he wouldn't have brought her along at all.

"Where do these all dump the feed to?" Cassidy asked as she scrolled through the information.

"A secure cloud that we, and Myke, can access. Which is why I want to put the street cams up first, so she can alert us if someone slips in behind us while we're in there."

"It looks like there's a four-man guard unit on site already, according to these images. Do we know their schedule?" Cassidy asked, then answered it herself. "Yeah, we do. It's right here. They do an outside walk around every three hours, but they're moving inside every hour. That makes sense. It's a fucking fortress and there's nothing important there – yet."

"Right, so nothing to really be guarding, or worrying about. They're just going through the motions right now," Chase said. "I've got the robots charged up and a couple of backup batteries plugged in in the rear of this thing. As long as we can get them set and secured quickly, we should be fine. It's not going to take us more than an hour or so to get these up."

Cassidy flipped through the screens, then leaned back and looked out the window at the passing scenery. "Putting them up isn't going to be the risk. Keeping them from being discovered and traced back to us – that's the risk."

"They're unmarked, and if someone did trace them, they'd show up as property of the FBIS," Chase said. "We're in the clear." He almost said 'don't worry' but that was patronizing and stupid to say to one of the top cops in the county, so he swallowed it down. He honestly didn't want her to have to worry, though. And that's when he mentally smacked himself. This is precisely why you don't date your subordinates. If he couldn't trust her to do her job while he did his, then what was the point in working together?

"We're here," he grumbled and pulled the Rover into a gravel cut-out where maintenance trucks could park when working in the area. He hit a button on the console and the windows went dark. There were no license plates anymore – all vehicles had digital tagging now – and one button blocked the tagging beacon from being read. The vehicle was now secure and anonymous. They unbuckled themselves, swiveled the seats, and got to work setting up the equipment. Ten minutes later, they each had a pouch with the tiny recording devices and a palm-sized robot that could climb buildings, poles, and in this instance – trees – to secure and activate the devices.

They pulled on the hoods that covered from the tops of their heads to where it sealed at the neckline, their faces obscured so an outsider couldn't see features, but the wearer could see perfectly without condensation or visibility impairments.

Outside the vehicle, they made their way to a tree that gave them an excellent view of the turn into the lab area. Chase gave Cassidy a nod and she sent the robot up the tree to secure the first device. The control was about the size of a small phone and Cassidy maneuvered the robot expertly. It was only moments before it was back down the tree and into her hand.

They crossed the road and went to the other side of the turn into the lab and repeated the process. Now it was time to put them up around the buildings. They'd discussed where to go and how to do it, then agreed to separate and each do a portion and meet at the Rover when they were done. Two clicks in the earbud meant there was trouble. A whispered 'done' was for when they got back to the vehicle. No talking otherwise, because they didn't know what kind of surveillance gear had been put up – if any – between satellite scans.

Myke spoke into both of their ears. "Confirmed, clear feed. You're good to go. Be safe, you two."

Cassidy went in one direction, Chase the other, as they slipped through the trees as silently as a hunter. They worked quickly and carefully, but it was a large area they had to cover, and they had to make sure each device was aimed properly because they couldn't really adjust them remotely. They were a one-and-done type of deal with a limited viewing range and a ten-year charge per device. That's why they had to set so many, so they could get as many angles as possible.

Chase hadn't used these in a couple of years and the differences in the older versus current model gave him some trouble, but by the third one, he was moving right along. He'd covered the front and the garage entrance, and was headed along the road that went from the garage entrance to the maglev spur when he heard two clicks in his ear and froze. Then he picked up the conversation – and her soft breathing. It told him what he needed to know as he slid through the shadows to get to the train garage.

The first batch went up just fine for Cassidy. She covered the back emergency exit and made her way to the train garage. She'd placed one in each upper corner of the garage entrance when she heard voices. The only place to hide was on top of the car currently on the track. Cassidy grabbed the side rail and pulled herself up, then reached the maintenance ladder that hovered just a few feet from the roof.

The voices got closer as she slid onto the curved surface and pressed herself flat, then keyed the recording in her hood to pick up what she was hearing.

"Are you sure the boss said you could use his place?" a male voice asked.

The sound of steps on the hard surface stopped. Another male voice spoke then. "You're questioning me?"

"N-no sir, but I have strict orders," the first man spoke again. "Let me call him and verify that you have permission – for my peace of mind, sir."

"I don't think so," the other voice said, then there was the sound of a choked cry and a wet, gurgling noise.

Cassidy turned her head and gave herself enough room to peer over the edge. A man in a khaki uniform lay on the platform below, his throat slit from ear to ear. Blood spread quickly and the killer stepped back to avoid getting the blood on his shoes. He crouched and wiped the blade on the dead man's pants leg, then folded the knife and slid it into his pocket.

She stayed where she was as the man picked up a fob from the ground near the body and pressed a button. A chirp sounded below her and the man smiled as he entered the train car. Cassidy stayed where she was, and whispered. "I'm okay, but on the roof of the train. Posted two recorders but not the rest. One guard dead on the platform. Will meet you at Rover as soon as possible."

Time passed and the faint rocking vibrations created from movement inside the train car had stopped. She hoped the man had gone to sleep or was otherwise engaged, so she started to work her way backwards to the ladder once more. She dropped silently to the platform opposite the body and hurried along the spur, where the shadows were deepest, to go further into the garage. She would place the last two recorders, then get out. The events of the evening had showed her the devices were needed more than they had suspected.

By the time Cassidy got to the Rover, Chase was past frantic and into the calm. When he saw her come out of the shadows and slip into the passenger side of the

Rover, he dove into the driver's seat and had them on the road before they'd even let the buckles finish fastening.

One hand pulled the hood off over his head and he let out a breath. "You're okay?" Chase finally asked, his hands fisted on the wheel.

"I'm okay," Cassidy replied, her own hood in her lap as her fingers massaged her scalp and fluffed her hair. "I think I recognized the man who killed the guard, but I want you to take a look first. Is Myke still connected?"

"Call Mykal Cutler," Chase spoke out loud.

"Calling Mykal Cutler," the AI voice responded.

"You two are okay, right?" Myke asked. "On the road, I see."

"We're fine. Tell me if you recognized the man that killed the guard?" Cassidy asked.

"Folsom Bentley," Myke replied. "Facial recognition identified both of them. Good job getting those first two recorders up. We've got it all on file now."

"Who was the other man?" Chase asked.

"Rocco Marzetti, a repeat offender for rape, aggravated assault, and so on. A real quality guard," Myke said, her tone dry.

Cassidy had seen dead bodies before, but she'd only seen one other person killed in front of her, and she needed a moment to process. She unzipped the front of her camo gear a few inches to get some air and let out a soft breath before she spoke. "Who kills with a blade anymore? I mean, that's up close and personal. Ninety-five percent of our murders are from pulse weapons or drugs."

Myke's voice softened as she spoke. "He's a sociopath, Cassidy. We've got two separate cases on him opened already, and now a third for this murder. You two get back to my place and I've got drinks, data – and Thai food. Come decompress for a bit, yeah?"

"Sounds good to me," Cassidy said, then glanced over at Chase.

"Yeah, sounds perfect," Chase said with a smile. "We'll be there in a few, Mykie. We're going to need a minute to change, though."

"Not a problem. See you in a bit," Myke said and signed off.

Chapter Seventeen

The three of them sat around Myke's little table and ate some of the best Thai food Chase had ever eaten. "You got this delivered?" Chase asked Myke.

"Yep. They use robot drone delivery. Drops it right outside the front door," Myke said around a mouthful of Pad Thai.

"I'll have to make sure to get the information from you. I see myself eating a lot of Thai food in my future," Chase said with a grin.

Cassidy ate, but she couldn't tell you what exactly she put in her mouth. She listened to the two friends talk and kept replaying the murder she witnessed just under two hours ago.

"What are we going to do about Marzetti?" Cassidy finally asked.

"Nothing right now," Myke said, then held up a hand to stop the argument she could see on Cassidy's face. A swallow of water and she sighed. "We didn't have a warrant to put up those cameras on the actual property. You guys were trespassing. The information we got – and will get – can only be add-ons after the fact. They cannot be the sole information used to get an indictment. But you know this."

"Yeah, I know this – but not doing anything and leaving a body behind goes against every instinct," Cassidy replied.

Chase wiped his mouth with a napkin and leaned back in the chair. "We don't want to screw up the other cases pending on Folsom, so we just watch and learn. It's not how I like to do things, either, but it's all we've got right now."

"I've been recording since you put up the street cams," Myke said. "I've got a van arriving about an hour after you left – then leaving again an hour or so later. I posted it so we can see where it goes."

"Folsom had someone come get the body and clean up the mess," Cassidy said as she picked at the noodles left on her plate.

"That's what I've deduced as well," Myke said. "Y'know, Cassie, you'd make a great analyst. Not many people can think outside the box like you've been doing."

Cassidy looked up at Myke in surprise, then gave a faint smile and shook her head. "Not for me. I don't think I could handle being behind a screen as much as you have to be. I got into being a cop because of the people."

"And you're really good with people," Chase said. "But Myke's right – you're also very good at seeing patterns others don't see. It's why I wanted them to make you chief and not me – because you have multi-faceted skills."

"You have them, too, Chase," Cassidy started to say and Myke interrupted them both.

"Personally? I think what they did when they chose the two of you for the positions you hold, it was very smart. Let's get blunt for a moment, shall we?"

"When are you *not* blunt, Mykie?" Chase grumbled and she shot him a toothy smile.

"Shut it, Payne-in-my-ass," Myke said, then continued. "Halstead was about as lined up with The Initiative as anyone could be. Women were kept down as much as possible. He arrange-married his daughter to Morris as part of an agreement with Morris's father. He murdered his wife because she was going to expose his crimes and report him to the FBIS. There were two – count them, *two* Black cops in the department, and two indigenous cops. That's it. Ellery and Bear Smythe. There was one woman to every six men, because that was federal law." Myke paused and got to her feet to grab the wine she had put in the fridge, two glasses, and a bottle of beer. When she sat back down, she hadn't stopped talking, just poured and passed out drinks. Beer for Chase, wine for herself and Cassidy.

"And here we have two people, equally qualified for the position of chief, but in different ways," Myke said. "Since you're dealing with a community that has, for nearly three generations, been run by men in the Halstead clan, it would be an easier pill for people to swallow to have a man as chief – albeit a Black man – than it would to have a woman. Making Cassidy your assistant chief gives her a step up if you ever decide to retire – and it also means the two of you can compliment each other with your different strengths."

Cassidy lifted her wine glass to Myke in a toast, then took a sip. "I hadn't thought about it like that, but you're right. It makes sense. For my part, I'm glad Chase is chief and not me." She looked over at him then and gave him a warm smile. "He's a lot more patient than I am. I probably would've kicked Bobo Fitch's balls up into his throat before I had the feds arrest him."

Chase had just taken a swallow of his beer when she said that and he choked on the mouthful, then barely got it down before he roared in laughter. "I would've paid to see that."

The room filled with laughter and banter – carefully recorded from two hundred yards up in the air where the drone silently hovered.

Folsom Bentley smiled as he looked over his evening's work. Every inch of the railcar was now wired for sight and sound – and tracking. He'd know who loaded the car, with what, and where it went. They were only using one car for now, to keep the traffic to a minimum and avoid discovery. Too bad for Rocco that he'd got in the way and tried to act like he was a real guard, for fucksake.

Folsom had to admit, though, the feel of the blade slicing through flesh was satisfying. He'd been getting itchy about needing another playmate, but Rocco had eased that itch for a little while. Speaking of playmates, it was about time to get rid of the last one – and he knew just how to do it in such a way that it served his purposes better than ever.

Before he was done, Folsom Bentley would be the mayor of this shithole county, and he'd be the one that soaked up a tidy chunk of profits from this lab. He was smarter than all of them, and he knew it. Now he just had to make it so that they paid him in credits, product – and power. His ultimate goal was to take over Milos Owens' position as head of Univy. Who better than the man who exposed Owens' failures and saved their precious lab while also boosting the lab's output?

He just had to be patient. Folsom wasn't great at patience, but he could manage it when necessary. For a little while.

Chapter Eighteen

The party at Myke's had wound down before dawn, and Cassidy was in no condition to drive herself home. Chase had an arm around her waist and helped her into his place, then took her into the spare bedroom.

There was a full-sized bed and mattress with dark gold sheets and a white comforter that waited for the duvet. Four pillows with gold and crimson pillowcases were fluffed at the headboard. A dresser, desk, and night stand were still in the boxes against the wall, but there was a chair next to the bed and that's where Chase put Cassidy.

"Let's get your shoes off and you can sleep it off here," Chase said as he crouched in front of her to undo her boot laces.

"I didn't know you had a guest room," Cassidy slurred, then closed her eyes. "Water, aspirin, bathroom. Please."

Chase pointed to the bathroom across the hall and Cassidy wove her way towards it, then shut the door. He put her boots under the chair and got to his feet, then went to get a couple of bottles of water for himself – and one to put on the chair beside the bed. He then went into his room and found a t-shirt he figured Cassidy could use as a sleep shirt and laid it on the bed.

"I put one of my shirts on the bed for you to use to sleep in," Chase said outside the bathroom door. "There's also another bottle of water on the chair. Yell if you need anything, okay?"

"Thanks, Chase," Cassidy called out and looked at herself in the mirror. It had been a long, long time since she'd overindulged in drink. She knew there were sober-up pills she could take, but they always made her feel sicker than just dealing with the alcohol. She washed her face and took a couple of the pain pills, then drank a large cup of water before she made her way back to the guest room. She shut the door to change and had to laugh when she pulled on the t-shirt. It was so large, she could've wrapped it around herself twice and still have enough to tie it off. She pulled a handful of it up at the collar and knotted it to keep it from sliding off one arm, then folded her clothes over the back of the chair and climbed into bed.

She closed her eyes and dropped into sleep, the wine – and the feeling of safety she got from being near Chase – enough to ease her quickly into dreams.

Light filled the bedroom where Chase slept, confusion clouding his brain when he woke to the smell of bacon and coffee. He paused at the edge of his bed, his sleep pants bunched up on one leg, and scrubbed his face with his hands. Yep, he still smelled bacon and coffee.

It wasn't until Chase had stumbled out into the hallway that he remembered Cassidy had stayed the night. Instead of greeting her with morning breath, he ducked into the bathroom to wash up and tend to his business.

"Good morning," he rumbled as he stepped into the main living space. "I thought I was dreaming when I smelled bacon and coffee."

Cassidy turned, a plate in one hand, a smile on her face – then she saw his bare chest and the ripple of muscles – and her mouth went dry. "Um, yeah. I hope you don't mind me taking advantage of your kitchen. I wanted to do something to thank you for the fantastic rest I got last night."

He couldn't have stopped his hand if he wanted to. Chase reached out and stroked her cheek. "Not sleeping well at home?"

"Not lately," Cassidy replied and took a step back to put the plate down on the counter. "Bacon is staying warm in the oven. How do you like your eggs?"

"Scrambled is fine," Chase said and reached for the coffee pot. The kitchen was small so the reach had put his chest up against Cassidy's back as she cracked the eggs into a bowl.

It flustered her so much she dropped the whole egg, shell and all, into the bowl. Her hands went to rest against the countertop as he paused with the coffee pot in one hand and a mug she'd set out in the other.

He leaned in and breathed in the scent of her hair, then whispered against her ear. "Am I bothering you, Cassidy?"

She felt the rumble of his voice as it moved through his chest, the brush of air as his words passed near her ear, and her legs trembled. She knew she'd regret it if she didn't make a move, then wondered – briefly – if she'd regret it if she did. That thought didn't stay for very long as she turned in the tiny space between his body and the counter, and reached up her hands to wrap around the back of his neck. Plastered to him, she pulled his mouth down to hers and feasted.

The coffee pot hit the counter, the cup hit the floor, and Chase's hands slid down Cassidy's back and filled his hands with her buttocks as he lifted her up. Those long, magnificent legs wound around his waist and Chase turned to sit her on the counter, his hands moving under the t-shirt of his she still wore.

Warm, smooth skin slid under his palms as he brushed them up her sides, then cupped her breasts where one thumb teased a nipple. He pulled the shirt the rest of the way up with the other hand and broke the kiss long enough to tug it over her head. His lips trailed down the side of her jaw, tasted the frantic pulse in her throat, then he found her breasts and feasted.

Cassidy nearly purred as he kissed his way down her body, her hands clutched at his shoulders as he tasted her skin. She needed more – more of him, more of this. His teeth gently closed around a nipple and she gasped, shocked by the bolt of pleasure – the sheer strength of it. She twined her legs tighter around him. "Bed. In your bed. I want to touch you."

The words took a minute to filter through the haze and he lifted his head to find her mouth once more. Hands cupped and lifted, arms wound around his neck as her legs wrapped his waist, and he carried her to his room. The blinds were drawn and the light painted lines across the blue sheets on his bed, then across the silken skin of the woman he spilled into them.

He reached for her panties – a scrap of black silk – and pulled them down her legs. His hands slid from ankle to knee before he lifted her and with one look at her face, buried himself in her core. Everything about her drove him mad. If a bomb had dropped on the house, he couldn't have stopped.

When she came, it hazed her vision and shook her body, her breath caught, then ragged as her heart raced. His hands were everywhere and when she gripped his biceps her nails bit in and he throbbed against her belly.

He thrust into her at last and for an instant, everything stopped – breath, sound, motion – then the wave of it pounded over them and he gave himself over to the sensations. When it swept through him, she broke beneath him, their hearts racing as bodies trembled and sighed.

There was no coherent thought, words wouldn't come, so Cassidy let the attempt go. She lay beneath him until he moved enough to pull her against him and give her the space to breathe.

It had never been like this for Chase. He had never lost himself so completely in a woman, to the point where he'd forgotten his own strength. A hand stroked down her arm and he quietly inspected for bruising, but the only bruise he found was the small one on her hip she'd earned from bumping the ladder on the train car. "I didn't hurt you, did I?" he finally asked.

She smiled first, then shook her head before she opened her eyes to look up at him. "Not even a little bit. That was...amazing." One hand stroked his cheek, the softness of his goatee under her hand as her thumb brushed his lower lip. Cassidy leaned up to kiss him – softly – sweetly – then she smiled and a glint of mischief lit her dark eyes. "My turn."

A hand pushed at his shoulder and he laid back on the bed, then watched as she straddled his hips and stroked her hands down his chest. Her hair brushed his skin as she leaned over and trailed kisses from the hollow of his throat to first one nipple, then the other. His hips bucked as she teased one with her teeth, then she slid lower still.

He tasted like soap and sweat and something she'd always equate to the essence that was Chase. She felt his muscles quiver under her lips and hands as she brought him back to life, then the soft cry of pleasure as she slid down over him. This time it was her turn to show him how much he pleased her – how much she wanted him.

The light moved across the room as they learned what pleased the other, what drove their lover to the heights of passion and sent them soaring over the cliff of release. They slept together, and Cassidy had no idea of the time when she slid from the bed to take a much-needed shower. The hot water beat on her skin and she reached for his soap when he stepped into the space and smiled.

"Let me," he murmured and reached for the soap. His hands caressed every inch of her body, as hers did his. They laughed and teased as they let the water rinse them clean, then wrapped themselves in towels to rescue the bacon from the oven and finish making their food.

Chase wore a pair of sweat pants and Cassidy had his robe wrapped all the way around her and tied with the belt. It hung to mid-calf and she had to roll the sleeves up to the shoulders in order to keep her hands free.

They were both laughing over a second cup of coffee when Chase's phone rang.

Another body had been found dropped in the forest.

Folsom felt he'd been particularly clever this time around. Just after he left the lab, he'd headed home and took the girl's body out of his freezer. The next day, in the early hours of morning, he loaded it into his heli. It took him only moments to change the registration reading of his heli to that of a heli owned by Milos Owens, then he lifted off from the green space behind his Pinehurst home and soared up over the forest.

The body had been purified and wrapped, so all he had to do was slice open the wrapping and tip the heli so she slid out through the cargo door. He'd wanted to do the same with Rocco, but it was easier to just have the van crew come get that one and scrub the platform clean.

This one was personal. He knew Owens had lost it with Nelson and Cragan – he'd heard the rumors already, and his contact had told him the cops were onto Owens for those. That's what had given him the idea to point the fingers at Owens for this one – and the other two he'd drop over the next few days.

He only had so much freezer space, after all.

Chapter Nineteen

Chase parked on the logging trail where Sergeant Angela Williams had dropped the pin for him to find her. She met him a few feet up the road and had him stop for a moment so they could speak. "Belfleur is at the site and he's been walking all over it and moved the body. I tried to get him to leave it alone, but he wouldn't listen."

"What the hell, Williams?" Chase shook his head. "No, I'm not angry at you. That little fucktard is going to regret this."

"I got photos and some measurements before he got there," Williams said. "One of my rookies tagged the site when a couple of hikers told him what they'd found. He was a few minutes out, so he came over and secured the scene and got the hikers to give a statement and their contact information. I got here about a half hour after he did and started to catalog the scene, when Belfleur showed up and did his best to fuck it all up. He tried to take my tablet, but I threatened to shoot him if he touched me."

Chase gave a wry chuckle. "I knew I liked you, Sergeant. Send the data to my tablet and I'll go have a word with our resident moron."

"Y'know, I figured after Halstead was gone, things would get better – and for the most part, they have," Williams said. "But it's guys like Belfleur that make me realize it's going to take a little longer to clean it all up."

"There will always be assholes, Sergeant. There was just a rather disproportionately large number of them in Lake County when Halstead ran things," Chase said. "And I can promise you that Belfleur is about to have a very bad day."

They both smiled at that as they turned to walk to the dump site.

Williams dropped back so she was behind Chase when he got to the line dropped by the first officer on the scene. The digital signature showed the original placement on Chase's tablet, and the new placement that was several feet from where it had been first placed.

Belfleur looked up and scowled when he saw Chase there. "We don't need you here, Detective."

"That's Chief to you, Ranger. Get away from my crime scene," Chase said, his tone flat and cold.

"Not your crime scene since it's on federal land," Belfleur retorted.

"Yes, it's my crime scene since I'm working these cases with the FBIS as lead investigator," Chase replied. "Now, get your ass over here, Belfleur. Now."

Belfleur stormed over to Chase and got right in his face, his voice a few decibels above normal speech as he screamed that Chase's mother had obviously whelped him in a kennel. Chase stood absolutely still until Belfleur poked a finger into his chest, then he moved like a coiled snake. His hand snapped out and grabbed Belfleur's hand, snapped the pointing finger to the side, breaking it at the knuckle, then dropped the man to his knees and spun him around until he was face first on the ground.

"Evan Belfleur, you are under arrest for assaulting a superior officer, corrupting a crime scene, and generally being a fucking asshole." He cuffed the man, dragged him to his feet with one hand, and marched him down the trail and away from the crime scene before he shoved him to the ground against a tree. "Sit. Stay. Even *you* should be able to manage that."

Chase then turned to Sergeant Williams and gave her a smile. "Sergeant, would you be so kind as to keep an eye on my prisoner while I call in my FBIS contact?"

"I'd be happy to, Chief," Williams said and turned to look down at Belfleur.

"He broke my fucking finger! I'm going to sue all of you," Belfleur screamed.

Chase dialed Red and put the call on speaker. "Senior Special Agent Jefferson, this is Chief Payne – you're on speaker. I've got Ranger Belfleur here under arrest, ready for FBIS pick up. Seems he assaulted me after he damaged a crime scene with another body dropped from the sky."

"What a fucking moron that ranger is. I'll be out there in about twenty minutes. Thanks for the call, Chief," Red said and disconnected the call.

Belfleur's face went from angry red to frightened white and he leaned back into the tree.

"Keep an eye on him, Williams. I'm going to see if I can salvage anything on this latest crime," Chase told her as he turned and walked back up the path.

Belfleur's footprints were all over the scene. The canopy had been broken through, as with the other two body drops, but this time the body was a naked young woman. There was something off about the way the body looked, so Chase moved a little closer and crouched down beside her. He noticed what looked like ice crystals in her eyelashes and in her hair – and bolted to his feet. His radio was in his hand before he'd fully stood and he was calling in a heli for the FBIS tech team and coroner.

"Tell them to rush it. The body was frozen prior to disposal."

That was all he needed to say to accelerate the pace on the other end of the line to warp speed. Every minute that a body was allowed to defrost would degrade the accuracy of any forensic measures. They needed to get the corpse suspended at the current temperature and hopefully keep any more evidence from being destroyed.

Chase really wanted to go back to Belfleur and punch him in the face, but he figured he could explain away the broken finger – but not punching a cuffed man into oblivion. He needed no further proof that Belfleur was on the payroll of whomever was dumping these bodies. Red would get it out of him. Chase trusted the experienced agent more than any other cop he'd known – including his father.

Red showed up and had two of his agents haul Belfleur off to a heli that would take him to a cell outside of DC, then made his way up to Chase as a team rushed past him with bags and gear.

"What's going on?" Red asked Chase.

"The body was frozen prior to dumping," Chase said. "She's defrosting quickly in this late summer heat and Belfleur fucked up the crime scene enough that we might never get enough to convict from this one."

"Well, shit," Red muttered. "That explains the medical heli and mass of Evidence Retrieval Techs all over the place. Good call to get them here so quickly."

"She's young, Red," Chase murmured as they stepped back off the path to give the ERT team some room. "And she looks like she was tortured and sexually assaulted. Bruising on her thighs and breasts."

"Folsom?" Red asked.

"That's what I'm thinking. You said to watch for this. Let's see whose aircraft were up over the forest in the past twelve hours, shall we?"

"I'll meet you at my place. I'm going to make a few calls to guarantee Belfleur a very...comfortable...stay in solitary so no one can get to him."

"Good idea. I'll see you in a few," Chase said and made his way back down the path. Sergeant Williams stood by her patrol vehicle and gave a wave to Chase, so he went to speak to her before he left.

"You did an excellent job, Williams," Chase told her. "I'll make sure a commendation goes into your file."

"Thank you, Chief," Williams said with a faint smile. "What's with the ERT rush?"

"The body had been frozen prior to dumping," Chase told her.

"That fu...er, sorry sir," Williams started to cuss and stopped.

"No, you're correct," Chase gave her a wry smile. "That fucktard piece of shit realized that and stalled things so we'd end up with damaged evidence. Don't worry, he won't be back. He's on a fast track to a cell outside of DC where the FBIS is going to pick his tiny little brain apart."

"What can I do to help, Chief?" Williams asked.

"Write up as detailed a report as you possibly can, and leave absolutely nothing out. Not one bit should be missed about what you saw Belfleur do and how he tried to take your official tablet. Get your officer to write up as detailed a report as well."

"We can do that, sir. Thank you, Chief."

"No, thank you, Sergeant Williams. If you want to stay here and help the FBIS team by answering any questions, feel free, but they have my information and SSA Jefferson's info, so you're free to leave."

"I'll stick around for a while and get started on that report," Williams said. "If they don't need me, I'll get back on patrol."

"Thank you, Sergeant," Chase said and went to climb into his truck. He started it up and pulled out of the chaos and onto the road before he spoke. "Call Cassidy."

"Calling Cassidy," the AI voice said.

"Hey, Chase. I'm just getting ready to leave your place. Did you need something?" Cassidy said.

"I needed to hear your voice," Chase replied with a smile. "If you're willing, could you head down to Red's place and join us for a meeting? This body dump was different from the others and I'd like you in on this."

"I got a change of clothes out of my duffel bag and cleaned up your place a bit. I can meet you at Red's. Do you need anything from here?"

"Just you," Chase said. "See you in a few minutes."

It was frightening how true those words were, he thought. Did he need anything? Just Cassidy. He'd never felt like this – not even, gods forgive him, with Janelle. They'd had passion and affection, and a deep appreciate for each other's intellect and skills – but this was more. So much more.

He couldn't stop the grin on his face as he drove back to Lakeridge and home.

Chapter Twenty

It was Red's pacing that told Cassidy something big was going down. She tapped on the patio doors and stepped inside when Red gestured to come in. Chase gave her a smile, then turned back to Red as Cassidy found a seat

"The best they can determine," Red said, "Is that the girl has been dead at least two weeks and flash frozen within twenty minutes of death. She'd been sterilized like the others Myke found on Folsom's trail – no DNA, hair, or fibers that didn't belong to the deceased – or weren't picked up falling through the trees and hitting the ground."

"That fits with Folsom's style, except for the body dump method," Chase said. "Do we have the flight list yet?"

"Myke's getting it," Red replied. "She'll send it to my wrist device when she has it. I've got her in DC, following up on Belfleur's arrest and seeing if she can get anything useful out of that idiot."

"Where's Folsom now?" Cassidy asked.

"At home in Pinehurst. We've had a car on his place off and on for weeks. He's rarely seen leaving and doesn't appear to get a lot of visitors," Chase said.

"What about his heli?" Cassidy leaned forward and pulled out her tablet. "One of the guys reported a heli landing behind his house and leaving an hour later. They said it was registered to Bentley, but that he was seen at home before it landed and after it left – so they assumed someone else had been using it."

"Is it registered to Bentley himself, or TechEd?" Chase asked.

Cassidy shook her head and tapped a message out on the table. "It doesn't say, but I've requested an update."

Red leaned on the back of the sofa and shook his head. "It doesn't matter who it's registered to because we didn't check to see if he even had access to a heli, just assumed he did but didn't have it stored locally. Now we've got another access point for him to use to avoid us."

A thoughtful look settled on Cassidy's face. "Did you have a car on him the night he killed Marzetti?"

"I think so?" Chase said as he pulled up the log for that night. "And they said he never left the house. Well, fuck. I guess I've been wasting the taxpayer's resources." He sighed and slumped back in the chair. "He's been playing us all this time."

"Can we drop a surveillance bubble on his house?" Cassidy asked. "I bet we could get Judge Endicott to sign off on it with what we've already got on him."

Red gave a brief nod. "Let's do it. Would it be better coming from me, or from you, Chief?"

"How about a joint request?" Chase replied. "I'll write it up and say it's part of a joint taskforce investigating the bodies being dumped in the forest. If that's not enough for the bubble, then we'll add on the other crap. This way it's clean and simple – and an already established case."

Cassidy reached for a bottle of water from the cooler bowl on the table, opened it and took a sip. "I know a surveillance bubble is a last resort kind of thing, but this guy has the resources and intelligence to slip by regular surveillance methods. The bubble will track if he flies out, tunnels out, drives out, or simply walks out. It'll keep a better eye on him than any patrol car could – granted, without the intimidation factor someone sitting there, staring at you, can offer." She took another swallow, then added. "Then again, the guy's a sociopath and isn't easily intimidated, so maybe pulling the manned surveillance will let him think he's getting one over on us."

Chase had pulled up a template document and filled it out, then handed the tablet to Red. "Here, you sign, then I'll send it over."

Red scanned the pages, added a note in two places, then signed the bottom. "I added case access codes, so the judge can read for herself. I know Gloria Endicott and she's thorough."

A tap, then another, and Chase put the tablet down. "Sent. Cassidy, you want to go ahead and pull the surveillance cars? He's getting around them anyway."

"Already did while you were doing the warrant request," Cassidy said while she stayed focused on her tablet. "I also opened up the cloud recording Myke set up for us and I'm scrolling back to just before we were there – to see if there was any traffic on the road in after we set up the cameras – and what traffic there was out. Now that we know about the heli, we've got more to look for."

"We know there were no vehicles that came in after we put up the cameras, or Myke would've told us," Chase said. "But we weren't looking at everything after that, either."

Red went into the kitchen and pulled down mugs. "You two want some coffee?"

"Gods, yes," Chase said. "Need some help?"

"Naw, I've got it," Red replied. "Cassidy?"

"Huh?" Cassidy said as she looked up. "What?"

"Do you want coffee?" Red asked.

"Yes, please. That'd be great," she replied and bent back over the tablet, fingers sliding across the surface, then a tap. When Red put a mug down on the table near her, she reached for it and handed him her tablet. "Look at tabs eight, twelve, and thirteen. Tell me what you see."

He put his own mug down, and reached for the tablet – then slowly sat. As Red looked over what she'd marked, Chase leaned in and Cassidy gave him a faint shake of her head.

"I don't want to color his impressions, so hold off a minute."

Chase gave her a smile and a nod. "Good point." He took a sip of his coffee and watched Red's face. He watched the expression of discovery light Red's face, then toasted Cassidy with his mug.

"He's changing the registrations on the heli, but it's all the same machine," Red spoke to Cassidy, respect and awe in his tone. "That scrape on the left cargo door is the same on each one."

"I started looking more closely at the heli's that landed in the clearing, and correlated their regs with the Flight Info tables – and noticed that while the machine looked the same, the numbers were definitely not the same."

Cassidy leaned over and tapped the tablet again. "He did the same thing here, but I'm not sure that's enough for an arrest."

"What do you mean?" Chase asked as he watched Red lean in.

"The heli that landed in his yard was registered to him," Cassidy said. "The next time one took off, two days later, it was registered to Milos Owens."

"And it was the same machine," Red murmured. "That brilliant fucker. No, it's not enough for an arrest, but once we get that bubble down, we can be more solid in what leaves and what lands and catch him at it again. Because you know if he's done it once, he'll do it again."

Chase looked over at them and gave a brief nod. "We can't prove that we didn't miss someone else landing, or something else taking off – without the bubble. But this explains why the last body was so very different from the first two. It's my suspicion that the first two were unplanned and either an accident or rage-induced, based on what I've learned about Milos Owens. This last one, however, was very different, and too carefully placed. It was clearly in the forest and close enough to Pinehurst to take time for us to get called in."

"And who would dump a body close to their home when they had other options? He's using the excuse of too obvious and stupid to keep us from looking his way," Red said. "Why don't you two head on out. I'll let you know if I hear from the judge. If she has any questions, Gloria will call me first."

"And if I hear from her, I'll let you know," Chase said. "Thanks for everything, Red."

Cassidy picked up her tablet and put her mug in the sink before she went over to Red and kissed his cheek. "You're my hero, Red. Stay safe."

"And you're a treasure, Cassidy," Red said and gave her shoulder a light squeeze. "Uncle Red is always here for any of you kids."

"We know that, and it's appreciated," Chase said as he led Cassidy out and shut the door behind him.

"Let's go back to my place and I'll cook this time," Chase said as they walked across the bridge and up the road to the village.

"Sounds like a plan," Cassidy replied. "Besides, I've got laundry going at your place." She plucked at the old band t-shirt she was wearing over a pair of faded jeans. "My last set of go-bag clothes isn't exactly the most presentable attire."

Chase chuckled and pulled her against him, then nibbled at her ear. "I prefer you without attire."

"Uh huh. You're not so bad without clothes yourself, but we need to talk about whatever this is that's going on here."

"Later. Food and laundry, maybe a nap, then serious discussion," Chase said.

"Is 'serious discussion' a euphemism for more sex?"

"Maybe."

Chapter Twenty-One

The office was dim with just a lamp on the desk and a lamp in the seating area offering circles of warm light. Milos sat at his desk, the holo chat up as he waited for Bentley to join the conference. Jonas sat on the sofa, a glass of vodka in his hand as he wasn't participating in the call but would be listening in – without Bentley knowing.

"He was a poor choice," Jonas said, then took a sip of his drink. "You knew it, I knew it, but the board outvoted us both. Now we've got to deal with his fuckups."

Milos took a sip of his bourbon, then put the glass on a small shelf below desk height. "Did you ever find that guard that went missing last week? Marzetti?"

"No, and it doesn't make sense," Jonas said. "He was on duty, went up to walk the train platform, and disappeared. His apartment was cleared out and there's been no activity on his phone or credit chips."

Milos frowned as he looked over at Jonas. "He'd been with DESCO a while, too, hadn't he?"

"Yes. Over five years. He was up for a promotion, too, so this is just..." Jonas stopped speaking when the chirp sounded that announced Bentley's connection.

"Good evening, Director Owens," Bentley said. "To what do I owe this pleasure?" He was wearing a black silk lounging robe, a gold chain, and his wrist device – and from what Milos could tell, nothing else. Bentley had done that on purpose, to show Owens how little he respected the man and his grasp on his power.

Milos wanted to tell the little fuck to go put some clothes on, but he recognized the power play and decided to simply ignore it. That should piss off Bentley and reset the scales a bit.

"Hello, Bentley. Your campaign for mayor is slipping and I'm not giving you any more credits until you actually do some work towards getting elected," Milos started.

Bentley shook his head. "You don't want to do that."

"Do what?" Milos asked as a faint smile curled his lips.

The robe gaped as Bentley leaned forward and snarled into the screen. "You don't want to threaten me like that. I can make your life hell."

"Speaking of threats," Milos said, his voice calm. "I think I'm going to take care of that now." He tapped on the controls on his desk top and Bentley flipped over his arm to look at the screen on his wrist device.

"You fucker," Bentley seethed. "You can't do this."

"Actually, I can. And I did," Milos replied. "Get your campaign in order and I'll turn the tap back on."

"You can't get anyone else in place to run. I'm all you've got."

"And if Ms. Foster wins, we'll figure out ways to put people in her administration and get our work done that way. You're not the *only* avenue, Bentley – just the most expeditious one."

Bentley slammed a fist on the table in front of him and leaned in to snarl at Milos. "I'm going to make you pay, Owens. Watch your back." Then the screen went dark.

"Well, then," Jonas said as he drained his glass and got to his feet. "Shall I activate plan B?"

Milos reached for his drink and took a swallow, his gaze thoughtful as he looked at the lights beyond the darkened wall of windows. "Let's give him a week and see what he does. If he doesn't move on the campaign front by Friday, then go ahead." He finished his bourbon and got to his feet to refill the glass. "Sometimes we make good decisions, sometimes we make bad ones. The key is knowing when to celebrate, and when to clean up the mess."

"Let your team know about the threats, Milos," Jonas said as he headed for the door. "Bentley may be a fucker, but he's brilliant and has the resources to cause you problems."

"I'll let them know. Thank you, Jonas."

Once he was alone again in his office, Milos sat down at his desk and logged in to an anonymous server. There were several files he'd been keeping on Folsom Bentley that might be of interest to the FBIS. He set them up to send on Friday – unless he entered a code to lock them back down. It was always wise to have a backup plan when dealing with a genius with no qualms when it came to doing everything it took to succeed.

He should know – he was one.

The surveillance bubble was in place over Folsom Bentley's house three days after the warrant had been signed. It should have given them access to all digital and physical traffic that went in and out of the space covered by the bubble, but there were issues from the start.

"Dammit, I should've expected this," Red swore as he worked in the corner of his main living space, the screens and console set in gleaming wood to fit in with the décor – and yet was more high tech than generally available in the public or private sector.

"Take a breath, love," Lacey soothed as she put a cup of coffee on the small table set nearby just for that. "He's supposedly a tech genius, I'm sure he could figure out a way to encrypt his transmissions and block listening devices."

Red reached up and took her hand from where it rested on his shoulder, and kissed her palm. "You're right, Lacey. You're right. I'm just frustrated." He closed his eyes and leaned into her torso as she stroked his hair with her fingers. "I don't like that this asshole is so close to you at times."

Lacey chuckled and kissed the top of his head. "Darlin', I've got assholes around me all day long. Trust me when I tell you I can handle them just fine."

Red turned and blew a raspberry into her shirt-covered belly and they both laughed. "Perhaps, love, but I'm your favorite asshole."

She cupped his face in her hands, then Lacey leaned down and gently kissed his lips. "I love you, Redmond Jefferson. And if you can't arrest this Bentley for something before the election, I'll just beat him anyway. I'm making stir fry for dinner, with snow peas like you like it. Go back to work and I'll be over here in the kitchen." She paused and rubbed a thumb against his cheek. "Tomorrow night, we're celebrating after the debate at my place – and we've got the whole place to ourselves because Grant is surprising Elle with a picnic at the new house."

"Doesn't he mostly live here with her anyway?" Red asked as Lacey moved away.

"He does, but he still pops in to use the holo-suite conferencing for work. Besides, that man has more clothes than I do, and Elle's little place can't hold them all."

The sound of real vegetables being prepared in his kitchen made Red smile. They preferred using raw food whenever possible to create meals together, instead of the scan-and-heat packaged stuff. He looked back at his screens and opened a new message. His mood improved dramatically as he turned to look over at Lacey. "Just got a message," he said. "Logan's on his way, but he has no furniture and was wondering if I had a cot he could use for a few days."

"Logan's coming? I'm sure Mary will be thrilled," Lacey said. "And I can make sure he has a couple of basic pieces of furniture and he can pick out others once he's here. When's he due in?"

Red watched her move around the kitchen as if she were dancing, her short auburn and silver hair catching the light. He really loved this woman – and loved the fact they had a good life they'd figured out together.

Lacey looked up and caught his expression, then gave him a smile and a wink. "Red, when's Logan coming in?"

"Oh, sorry. I got lost in watching you – again," Red said and got to his feet. "He's hoping to be here by Saturday. He bought a truck and is camping in the back of it. He wants to stop and visit Maggie and Kate and their families, and see the sights before he gets here." Red wrapped his hands around Lacey from behind and kissed her neck, then stepped out of her way so she could work. "Thomas has never forgiven him for not going into the Catholic priesthood and instead choosing Episcopal – as if one path to a person's god is better or worse than another."

"Thomas has always been a sanctimonious, self-right-eous prick," Lacey said. "And Mary doesn't have enough backbone when it comes to her children to give a worm pause." She stopped and pulled her lips in, then turned to Red. "My saying that isn't very kind, is it? I'm just tired of people hurting their children because they think they've got a right. Every single one of those kids left home the minute they could, and only Logan has come back once a year to visit his mother because Thomas won't let her go anywhere without him." She slapped the cover on the rice steamer and turned to look at Red. "And then, he stays at my place because Thomas won't let 'one of those pissant priests' stay under his roof."

Red stepped up and pulled her into his arms. "You've been a mother to every single one of those Chess Club kids since the day Grant brought them over for practice. What do you say we get online and get Logan set up while we eat? We can pick out things together and get him started building a home of his own."

Lacey kissed him and patted his cheek before she turned back to her dinner prep. "That sounds perfect. I have some idea of what he likes from when he's stayed with me, and you've seen him once or twice at his place in Wilmington, right?"

"I don't know if that counts," Red said. "It was a suite of rooms in a shared house with other members of the church community. He had a bedroom, a small sitting room-office combo and a private bathroom. There was a micro kitchen in one corner of the sitting room and that was it."

Lacey stirred the strips of beef in the pan and shrugged. "Okay, then we'll go with neutrals and let him add what he wants as he goes. Would you get the plates down?"

By the time they'd finished eating, Logan's place had everything from dishes and cookware to bedding, towels, and the much-needed furniture.

"That was fun. Thank you for sharing that with me," Lacey told Red. "Now, in the spirit of sharing, I'll wrap up the leftovers and you can do the dishes?"

Red chuckled and got to his feet. "As you wish, my love."

"Yep, you're a keeper," Lacey laughed. "Quoting lines from one of my favorite old movies."

Red helped clear the table, then leaned in to kiss her cheek. "Another hour or so of work and I can come watch it again with you. Sound good?"

"Sounds like perfection," Lacey said.

Chapter Twenty-Two

Cassidy was home long enough to grab a few things and kiss her Doda's cheek. She dropped the bags in her vehicle and went back inside to check the fridge and the food supply.

"Doda, do you need me to order you groceries today?"

"No, I'm good," Sid said. "You're working so much with this promotion, Cassidy. Or is it something else?"

Cassidy gave her father a sweet smile and bit her lower lip. "I'm in a relationship with a man, Doda, but I'm being very careful. I don't want to move too fast, and there are complications that we have to sit down and figure out."

"You are a strong, beautiful woman, Cassidy. Don't let any person dim your shine. Not a romantic partner, or anyone else – including me," Sid said as he reached out for her hand. "Do what you head and your heart tell you, and I will be happy that you are happy. That's all any parent wants for their child – a good and happy life."

"Thank you, Doda," Cassidy leaned down to kiss his cheek. "I love you. Call me if you need anything, yes?"

Sid grinned at his daughter. "Or I can call Sariah Windwalker. She's been bringing me meals and staying to share them with me."

"Go get 'em, Doda," Cassidy said with a laugh. "Sariah is a beautiful soul and beautiful to look at. I won't be home unless you call for me. Enjoy, my beloved father."

A huge smile settled on Cassidy's face as she got into the vehicle and drove towards Chase's place. He'd given her space in his closet and a couple of drawers in his dresser, and all but asked her to move in with him. Their routine had settled into going into work separately as they often needed their vehicles during the day, then once at home, taking turns cooking. Although, she had to admit Chase was better in the kitchen than she was.

She parked beside Chase's vehicle and started to unload her things when she heard a faint whining noise. A glint of shadow and light against the top of a pine tree caught her eye and she reached into her gear bag for her scope and brought it up to her eye.

"Chase!" she yelled. "Get out here."

Chase had just shoved his feet into his sneakers when he heard her yell, so he raced out the door and skidded to a stop. "What? What's wrong?"

"Got your long-range weapon?" Cassidy asked.

"In my truck. Why?"

"There's a drone stuck at the top of that tree over there. If you can tag it, we can maybe figure out who the fuck's been spying on us."

Chase went to his truck and in a few moments had his long-range weapon in his hands. He sighted in on the drone and took aim – then fired. The drone shuddered and spun with one of the propellers shot out, then dropped from the tree to the ground.

Cassidy was already running and got to the drone as it landed in a pile of pine needles and brush just past Zach's future home. She grabbed a stick and pulled the drone out of the brush, then held it up on the end of the stick towards Chase.

Chase grabbed the drone and popped the back off of it with a pocket knife and pulled out the data chip. "Now they can't erase it, if they haven't already. Let's go see what we caught."

They carried the gear and Cassidy's things inside, then Chase pulled out a device that allowed one to scan and read a chip without plugging it into the network. He smiled as he read the information, then handed it to Cassidy. "Looks like we got us a live one."

While she read the information, Chase called Red and explained what had gone down. "He's on his way up. So, Fitch decided to get sneaky, huh?"

"I'm not surprised," Cassidy said. "But this is a problem for us. We haven't filed the relationship status paperwork with the state yet. They could use his information and fire us both."

"Information he gathered illegally? He won't take it anywhere," Chase said. "But we should get online and file that paperwork anyway. Want to talk about it after Red's done?"

Cassidy gave him a nod and stacked her things out of the way, then went to make a pot of coffee. She was worried that they'd started something they couldn't continue – not and keep their jobs. And there was no way in hell she was quitting over a relationship, no matter how amazing the relationship was. Nor did she want him to have to quit, because he was so good for the department – and the county. It broke her heart, but they might have to go back to just being friends. Cassidy didn't know if she could do that. Not now that she knew how his hands felt on her skin and his lips on her...

"Can I come in?" Red called out.

"Yeah, come on in. Cassidy's getting coffee," Chase said from a seat at the table where he was scrolling through data on his tablet. "Drone's registered to Beauregard Fitch, an officer I fired a week after I took the chief job."

"Fitch...Fitch...wait, isn't that Montgomery's son?" Red asked.

"Yep," Cassidy replied as she set the mugs of coffee down. "And he used that connection every time he was disciplined about something. I swear if I heard "my Daddy will" out of his mouth one more time, I might've just punched him in the throat."

"And he now has documentation about you two having a relationship outside of the usual friendship boundaries, yes?" Red asked with a glint of humor in his eye.

"A relationship we have yet to report to the state bureau yet," Cassidy murmured as she kept her gaze on her coffee mug.

"A relationship we'll report as soon as we're done talking to you," Chase added and reached out for one of her hands. He paused when she didn't give it to him right away, then turned back to Red. "Unless you have another idea?"

Red watched the interplay and felt he had a pretty good idea of what was going on. "Both of you, look at me, please." He waited until Cassidy's eyes were on his face before he smiled. "I've watched the two of you fall in love with each other these past weeks, and it's a beautiful thing. Don't let rules and regulations keep you from the one person in your life that makes it all worthwhile." He leaned back and picked up his coffee. "Do you realize there are over eleven hundred partnered couples working in the same department, often on the same shift, in the many different law enforcement and first responder organizations in this country?"

Cassidy's eyes widened and she reached for Chase's hand. "Seriously? That many?"

Red nodded. "That many. And with that kind of precedent, I don't think the two of you have anything to worry about. On top of that, Judge Endicott and I have both put letters of recommendation and commendations for exemplary service in your files – since you took your new positions."

"Thank you," Chase said, his voice rough as he looked at Red.

"There's more," Red said with a wicked grin. "Bo Fitch is a registered member of The Initiative and as such, he will be picked up and held for an indeterminate time after breaking his parole with the FBIS. We released him a few days after we'd picked him up and apparently, he started stalking the two of you. If you hand over that drone and chip, I'll see that he's sent away for a good long time. Well, long enough that you two will likely forget about him before he gets out again." Red finished his coffee and put the mug aside. "I had myself a nice long chat with Montgomery after the first arrest, and he's fed up with, as he put it, his idiot son. Meaning, there will be no backlash on you from that quarter, either." He got to his feet and took the chip out of the reader, then picked up the drone. "Good shooting," he said to Chase and left them both seated at the table as he went out the door.

They heard him whistling as he walked down the road, then turned to each other.

"I was going to..." Cassidy started, while at the same time Chase spoke.

"We can," he paused and looked at her. "You want to go first?"

"I was going to ask to be reassigned to the Pinehurst station and still act as your second, but that would give us distance and hopefully not get us fired," Cassidy said.

"No," Chase said. "I don't want you that far away." He smiled and lifted the hand he still held, then kissed her fingers. "In fact, I want you to completely move in here with me. I want you to see if you can live with me and maybe think about being my partner."

"What about Janissa?"

Chase held her close and kissed her forehead. He'd told her about Janelle and Janissa the day they'd come back after getting the warrant sent out for the surveillance bubble. "I think she'll be just fine with it. She's been wanting me to find someone to make me happy." He paused, then laughed low. "She also wants a brother or a sister."

"Well, we'll have to talk about that later," Cassidy replied with a chuckle. "There's plenty of time for that." She leaned in against him and sighed. "On my drive over here today, I was so very happy. I know we're going to have to work through some logistical stuff with the job, but you, Chasen Payne, make me happy."

"And you make me happy. I thought I loved Janelle, but this is so much more. It's different and in a good way. Stronger."

Cassidy sighed softly and buried her face in his neck, then kissed him there. She felt him shiver a little and grinned. "I love that I can make you do that. Now, before I completely distract us both, let's get that form filled out."

Chapter Twenty-Three

Chase loved waking beside Cassidy. He watched her sleep, her features relaxed and at peace. He lifted a strand of hair from her cheek and breathed in the scent. Soft, silky, and fragrant, he rubbed the strands between his fingers, then slid them back so he could brush her cheek. Her eyelashes fluttered and he smiled.

"Good morning, beautiful," he rumbled.

"Good morning," Cassidy murmured as she snuggled into him. "What time is it?"

"Not time to get up yet. Soon, but not yet," Chase replied as he slid his hands down her bare back and along one thigh. She opened to him so easily as his fingers found her already wet and ready for him. He teased her body awake before he slid her on top of him and tasted her lips, her throat, then her breasts. Her body was his to explore, to savor and sample with soft kisses and gentle touches.

Thorough, she thought dreamily, and oh so patient. Here was a partner who sought to please as much as he took pleasure, to give as much as he took. He was the first lover she'd ever taken that made her body quiver and her breath catch – and because of that, she gave him more. Her hands caressed the warm planes of muscle and sinew that held such power and could be so gentle.

"Let me," Chase rumbled as he pressed a hand to her core and watched her eyes go opaque and her skin flush, a rose hue under the dusky satin. The sound of her cry made his thighs tense and she gasped and reached for him.

"Chasen. Chase," she repeated and shifted so he slid into her.

The sheer pleasure of filling her shot through him like a rocket, having the wet heat of her around him. It took every ounce of control to move slowly and savor each gasping rise and each trembling fall of their bodies. He watched the pulse beat in her throat as her body arched back and the pleasure built stroke by deep, slow stroke. They clung to the edge, and when he felt her clutch around him, he pulled her down to meet his mouth and they took the fall together.

"I could get used to this," Cassidy said as they showered together. Gentle touches and lathered caresses, and a deep, slow kiss were shared before they dried off and got dressed for the day.

Chase was making them breakfast while Cassidy made the bed and straightened the room. The late summer weather had had him open the French doors to the screen porch so the scents of the morning could drift in on the light mountain breeze.

That's where Myke tapped when she saw the doors open. "Can I come in?" she called out.

"Come on in, Mykie," Chase replied and pulled out another mug for coffee. "Have you eaten yet?"

"Yeah, I'm good. Grabbed a breakfast sandwich at Red's when I debriefed. He said I should come up here and fill you in on what I've learned." She dropped into a seat at the table and accepted the mug of coffee, then added a healthy splash of cream.

Cassidy came out and smiled at Myke. "Hey, you. I like that shade of purple. Did you refresh it?"

Myke ran a hand over the top of her hair and grinned. "Yeah, I wanted something darker for a change." She looked from Cassidy to Chase and sighed. "I'm so glad you guys figured out your shit. You both look beyond happy."

Cassidy laughed and took her mug from Chase before she joined Myke at the table. "I am happy. Besides, what kind of idiot would I be to pass up a man who cooks?"

"I know, right?" Myke retorted and Chase rolled his eyes. "Okay, so I had Belfleur in a cell outside of DC and once he realized his ass really was on the line, he sang like the proverbial bird."

"Was he singing about Bentley?" Chase asked as he slid a stack of waffles onto the table, along with fresh-cut berries, homemade whipped cream, and a warmed pitcher of syrup. He winked at Myke when he put three plates and utensils out as well, knowing she couldn't refuse his waffles.

"Yeah, okay, I'll have one," Myke said as they filled their plates. "And yes, he sang about Bentley. But he also sang about Milos Owens. Seems Bentley and Owens have an arrangement where Owens fronts the costs and Bentley gets the mayoral seat by buying votes – then smooths the way for the medical facility to also front as a drug lab."

"We'd figured out some of that," Cassidy said. "About the lab at least. But not that Owens was giving Bentley the credits to buy his election."

"It's not that far of a reach, though," Chase said as he took a bite of waffle.

"No, it's not. Not when we know Univy bought Bentley's company. The problem is, we have no proof, just Belfleur's word, which isn't worth much," Myke said. "It confirms some of what we'd figured out, and gives us a direction to look, though."

Cassidy swallowed a mouthful of waffle, berries, and cream and sighed. "So damned good." A sip of coffee and she added. "We got a surveillance bubble put over Bentley's place after we learned that he was changing the registration on his heli so it looked like it belonged to Owens. Since the bubble's been set, he's behaved. We've only got him coming and going to events where he talks about bringing the county back to basics."

"Oh, gods, one of those?" Myke sighed. "Let me guess, where men were men and women knew their place?"

"Yep," Chase replied. "And some of the pro-Halstead residents are eating it up."

Myke finished up her waffle and leaned back with her coffee. "That was excellent, Chase. Thank you. Now, I'm going to finish this coffee, go home and get some sleep. After I get some rest, I'm going to dig in to Milos Owens and that lab. I want to see what permits and notices they've filed for the place and I want to see what other connections Owens might have out this way."

"You never know what thread you pull that might lead to a big fish," Chase told her and looked over at Cassidy. "We're going to finish up with Janissa's room. I know you said you'd help, Myke, but you've been more than a little busy."

"Crap, I forgot about that. I'm sorry, man. Yeah, you two figure it out," Myke yawned and put the mug down. "Here's the link to the set I found that I thought she'd like." She dropped the link from her wrist device to Cassidy and Chase's, then got to her feet. "I'm gonna go before I start snoring on your table. Catch you guys later."

Once Myke had left, Cassidy shook her head. "She's going to burn out if she doesn't slow down a little. I mean, she's amazing, but how many balls can one woman keep in the air at one time?"

"With Myke?" Chase said with a chuckle. "As many as she wants. She's absolutely brilliant and seems to thrive on chaos."

"You cooked, I'll clean," Cassidy said as she started to clear the table. "Then let's bring up that set and take a look at it. I also want to get a couple of throw rugs and some cute lamps. We don't want to get too much, though, because she'll want to make it her own space with her own touches."

"I think you two will get along great. She's supposed to be here Saturday night, so I figured we could go for a hike on Sunday up to the waterfall. She loves hiking but there's no real place for it in Chapel Hill."

"I'm looking forward to it," Cassidy replied. "Okay, let's get shopping. You can put it on the big screen so I can see while I clean up."

They decided on the bedding and curtain set that Myke had chosen. It was in shades of green, blue, and gold with Celtic knotwork and tribal designs on the duvet cover and the border of the curtains. A couple of throw pillows in the same shades of green and blue, soft braided rugs of blue, gold, green, and cream echoed the color scheme and softened the plank-style floors. A pair of lamps and a cushion for the chair finished the order. By the time they were done, the kitchen was clean and they were seated on the screen porch with their tablets and a pot of coffee. Even though it was a day off for them, they still had some work they could get done.

Cassidy looked up at Chase as he worked and smiled. This life? This she could get used to. In fact, she planned to get very used to it all.

Chapter Twenty-Four

The debate had been scheduled for a couple of weeks, so Lacey was ready when Thursday evening rolled around. She stood at the podium in a dark blue skirt suit and cream silk blouse with garnets at her ears and on her wrist and a simple silver necklace that settled a teardrop garnet that settled just below the collar of the blouse. Her shoes matched her suit and put her at eye level with Folsom Bentley when they met in the middle of the platform to shake hands.

His white blonde hair was combed back and he looked vaguely anemic against the dark gray suit and pale blue shirt he wore. They returned to their separate podiums and the monitor began the questions. The first two went well, but the third question is where it started to fall apart.

"If you are elected," the monitor read. "What is the first order of business you will address as mayor?"

It was Lacey's turn to answer first and she smiled into the recording lens before she spoke. "As mayor, it is my duty to see to the needs of the people in Lake County. The people of this county have had their homes and land stolen by corporate thieves, their lives disrupted by illegal drugs, and their livelihoods threatened by organizations determined to take over small businesses and replace them with conglomerate box stores. I will fight that kind of destruction and do my best to make sure our way of life improves with appropriate measures, not heavy-handed tactics."

Folsom made a rude sound of amusement and tsked softly. "Dear woman, you have no idea what it takes to run a business, so of course you'd be against the processes and procedures a business takes to succeed. When I'm elected mayor..."

"I'm sorry, Mr. Bentley, but you're wrong," Lacey said. "I helped my husband run Foster Consolidated for over twenty years, then ran it while my son finished his education for another five years before I worked with him to help turn it into a successful business both on and off planet."

"I'm never wrong," Folsom snapped. "You're a fucking idiot, but then you're a woman, what could we expect?"

"Mr. Bentley, do you need a minute to calm down?" the monitor asked. "Because speaking to Ms. Foster like that is against the rules."

"I don't need to calm down," Folsom shouted. "I need to not have to waste my time standing up here while that woman babbles about shit she doesn't even understand. I'm done. If you want an imbecile for a mayor, go ahead and vote for her. If you want someone who can bring progress to this backwater hole, then vote for me." He turned from the podium and shoved his way past a couple of the recording crew and out the door.

"I think we can end the debate now, yes?" Lacey said with a wry smile. "Unless you want to ask me the questions and I can continue to answer for the people watching to hear more?"

"Your platform and information have already been published, Ms. Foster. We'll just post it up after the break. Thank you for your time and your patience," the monitor said.

"Thank you, sir," Lacey replied and stepped away from the podium. Her bodyguards appeared on either side of her and one went to the door while the other handed her her purse.

"Let Joe check the parking area and have Tom bring the car around before we go out. That nutjob might be out there," Rick said as he stood with Lacey.

"Of course," Lacey said and pulled out her phone to call Red. She smiled when she saw his face on her screen. "Did you watch?"

"I did. Are the guys making sure you're safe?" Red replied.

"They are. Rick is here with me, Joe is checking the parking area and Tom's bringing the car around." She took a breath and let it out slow. "You said he was a sociopath. I didn't realize just how unstable he truly was. I hope people see this tonight and decide he's in no way fit for public office."

"They might see that, or they might see someone with their same beliefs and frustrations," Red reminded her.

"I have to believe they want something other than that," Lacey replied. "Joe's back, I'll be home soon."

"Come here tonight. I'd sleep better knowing you were beside me," Red asked and Lacey smiled.

"I'll sleep better knowing you're beside me, too – while he's still out there." She blew him a kiss and disconnected the call.

Joe sat up front with Tom while Rick got into the back with Lacey. They locked it down and pulled out of the lot while Lacey leaned back and closed her eyes. The reinforced vehicle made her feel safe since she knew neither a bomb, missile, or pulse weapon could penetrate the exterior.

They hadn't taken into consideration a sociopath with the ability to interfere with the signal between the vehicle's computer and the satellite link they all used for location and security systems.

"Something's wrong," Tom said as he tried to keep the car on the road. "It keeps trying to turn on me."

"Is something interfering with the signal?" Joe asked as he tried to shut down the external link. "I can't shut down the tracking system."

Rick turned to Lacey. "Call Red, then hold on tight." He pulled down another control panel and tried to help Joe break the connection. "It's being controlled from outside the car."

Red answered the call, but Lacey didn't give him a chance to speak. "First off, I love you. Second, the car is being controlled from outside. The men are trying to break the connection and Tom's trying to keep us on the road, but it's not working. Triangulate my phone so you can find us."

"The car is able to withstand a drop off a cliff, Lacey. You might get some bruises, but the inflation system will protect all of you. Just don't open any of the doors until I get there with a team."

"I hear you, Boss," Joe said from the front. "Don't leave us out here too long, okay?"

"I'm on my way, everyone. Do your best and stay calm," Red said loudly enough for all four to hear. "Now, Lacey.

Tuck your phone under your leg and cross your arms to hold each strap handle on your buckles. That'll keep you from smacking yourself in the face when the inflation system goes off. I love you, baby. See you soon."

Rick leaned back and tucked the control panel back into place, then crossed his arms and gripped the strap handles. "Let's ride this bitch down, everyone. Tom? Let it go. If we go here, the drop isn't as far as it is further on and we'll be in an easier place for rescue to get to us. Hold on and close your eyes."

Lacey watched Joe grip the handles, then Tom as the car jerked to the side and scraped over the guardrail before it sailed into the air and landed about a hundred yards down the cliff. The inflation system filled the car and held each person in place as the vehicle rolled several times before it finally came to a stop on its side, then shuddered and slammed back onto the wheels.

Once it stopped moving, the inflation system deflated and they all took a breath.

"Everyone okay?" Tom asked, his voice shaky.

"I'm good," Lacey said. "But I'm never going on a roller coaster again."

They all laughed in relief and Joe glanced out through the windshield. "There's someone out there, on the cliff. I'll let them know we're okay." He started to open the door and everyone shouted at him to stay inside and shut the door.

He shut it pretty fast when a long-range pulse blast hit the top of the door frame and sent sparks flying. "Not a friendly," Joe muttered as he held the door shut.

Lacey pulled out her phone and noticed Red was still connected. "We're all okay, at the bottom of the cliff about five miles north of the studio. Someone's up on the road with a pulse weapon and they just took a shot at us."

"I've got a team almost there. Stay in the car," Red said. He was in his heli, and knowing someone was shooting meant he couldn't land nearby. He called in the shooter to his team and they split up with one group coming on from either side.

It was the longest fifteen minutes of his life while he hovered out of range of the weapon and watched the flashes of light as the shooter took pot shots at the car.

The team arrived and took down the shooter with little fanfare, then Red landed the heli on a patch of ground about twenty yards from the car. He was out before the motor quieted and ran to the car to pull the back door open. Once Lacey was in his arms, he felt like he could finally take a deep breath.

"We're all okay, Red. We are. I could just use a shot of whiskey and a soak in the hot tub. What do you say?" Lacey said with a smile, one hand on his cheek.

"I say that sounds like heaven," Red replied.

Chapter Twenty-Five

Milos read the news files as they scrolled across his screen. Bentley's performance at the debate had the public in an uproar. His ranking dropped to three percent and Owens wanted to kick something. Instead, he added a shot of whiskey to his morning coffee, then brought up his message screen and hit send. The files on Bentley were now being sent to the FBIS agents handling the investigation into the bodies dropped in the forest – and they were all now laid at Bentley's feet. He had also added a bit about his parents and grandparents, and some information about how many young women had disappeared after being sent to Bentley's place for a private party.

Milos hoped Bentley survived in prison long enough to really suffer. Now he had to figure out who he could buy that would be in Lacey Foster's administration. He had people that were good at research -they'd come up with something.

Chase read the report from the night before that Red had shared with him, then pulled up the files and wrote up what information he had on the shooter to send back to Red.

"What are you working on?" Cassidy asked as she slid a sandwich on a plate next to his tablet.

"Red sent me the report on the shooter from last night, and the FBIS is going in to pick up Bentley – if they can find him. He's not at his place right now. Didn't come home last night."

"Who's the shooter?"

"Remember that officer, Gordy Reed? A cousin of the Halsteads, I think. He left on his own after the Halsteads were picked up, and got a job in security somewhere. Well, apparently Bentley paid him to try and kill anyone who got out of the car once he'd wrecked it."

"I remember Reed. He was a few slices short of a sandwich," Cassidy said. "The only reason he was on the force was his relations."

"Do you have a private file on him I can add to the official report for Red?" Chase asked.

Cassidy pulled out her tablet. "I think I do. I kept files on behavior issues and criminal activity, and kept it on my private cloud server." She tapped a few times, then sent the file over to Chase. "Here you go."

Chase worked for a moment, then sent the file and leaned back to eat his sandwich. "You ready to go get Nissa?"

"I'm all set. Her room is ready and all I need to do is put my shoes on," Cassidy said. "How's she getting here again?"

"Red's got an agent flying in to help with the Bentley case, so they picked up Nissa at her grandparent's place and will land on Red's pad. We just have to walk down and meet her."

"Then let's go," Cassidy laughed and tugged his arm. "I don't want her to be standing there, waiting on us."

"No, you'd rather we stood around and waited on her," Chase grumped, then grabbed Cassidy and spun her around. "I'm eager to see her, too. Let's go."

They got to the landing pad on top of Red's barn just as the heli came in to land. Agent Ophelia Winslow got out of the craft, then turned to open the back cargo area and started to haul out luggage.

On the other side, a tall, slender girl with long dark braids and sable-hued skin got out in a rush and raced to Chase. She launched herself and Chase caught her in his arms and hugged her tight. "I've missed you, Nugget."

"Oh, Papa, I've missed you too. And I'm not nugget-sized anymore, you should just call me Nissa," Janissa chided him with a grin. She turned to look at Cassidy and asked. "Hugger or not?"

"Hugs are great," Cassidy replied with a chuckle and Janissa wrapped her arms around her and gave her a solid hug.

"I've got to help Fee with my stuff. She said I had too much and we'd need to do it in two trips," Nissa said, then paused to look back at Chase. "She was teasing, but I did bring a lot."

They all went over to sort out the luggage and Chase shook Fee's hand. "Thank you, Agent Winslow. I appreciate you delivering all of the baggage – and my daughter – to us safely."

Fee laughed and tugged on one of Nissa's braids. "It was my pleasure. No, really it was. You all enjoy your time together. I've got to head down and get to work. See you later."

Chase took one look at the pile of luggage, then grabbed a few cases then went down the stairs. "We're borrowing the cart to get this all up to the house."

Nissa took in her surroundings with an attention to detail Cassidy admired in one so young. "Look, a cat on the balcony," she pointed to Quinn who was perched on the upper level of Ellery's screen porch.

"That's Quinn, Ellery Adler's cat. He's a sweetheart," Cassidy said.

"Why are there so many recorders around?" Nissa asked. "Is this place that high security?"

"It is. It's not just home to people that work in law enforcement, but it's also where some of them do their jobs," Chase explained. "Equipment and gear are also stored here, so security is necessary."

A firm nod of her head and Nissa smiled. "I'm glad. I feel safer here, already."

"Wait, do you not feel safe at your grandparents' place or at school?" Chase asked as he pulled the cart up to the house.

"Not so much," Nissa said as she grabbed a couple of her bags. "I can tell you more about it over a cold soda?" Nissa asked as she followed Chase inside.

Cassidy grabbed the last two bags and shook her head. That girl was going to keep Chase – and herself – on their toes. In a good way.

Chapter Twenty-Six

Janissa had her own agenda and she was well on her way to making it happen. She loved her new room and the thoughtful theme and color scheme. Some of the stuff she'd brought was to decorate the room, so she went about doing that while she put her clothes away. She'd popped in her earbuds and had music playing that made her want to dance while she worked, so she didn't notice Cassidy in the doorway until she caught the wave of the woman's hand.

A tap on the buds and she quieted the music with a laugh. "Sorry," Nissa said. "I had my music up. Did you need something?"

Cassidy watched the girl dance and felt a warmth settle in her chest. "I just wanted to check in and see if there was anything you needed that we'd missed. I had almost forgot closet stuff and it just came in this morning, so I made sure to tuck it in there."

"Everything's great so far," Nissa replied. "I'm used to a smaller space at school, so I'm enjoying having room to spread out."

She'd caught the hesitation in Nissa's voice, so Cassidy stepped further in and shut the door. "Sounds like something's not so great about school," she said. "Want to talk about it?"

Nissa gave a half-hearted shrug as she folded a pair of jeans and put them in a cubby in the closet. She thought about what she could say or how to explain it, then turned and sat on the bed and patted the spot beside her for Cassidy to sit.

"I'm not sure how to say all of it, but I'm hoping you can help me explain it to Papa," Nissa said. "School is school and I'm still top of the class, but I don't like being away from my family so much, and while Memaw and Pops are great, they're older and slowing down and can't do the things I'd like them to do, like take me to events and stuff. A kid needs parents for that."

"What would you like, then? How do you want to change it?" Cassidy asked.

With those words, Janissa realized Cassidy was going to be a fantastic mother. She let out a soft breath and smiled. "I want to stay here, with you and Papa. I can still attend classes at the Academy online, or go to school around here, but I'm tired of feeling lonely, or like I don't matter."

Cassidy's heart broke for the girl and she put an arm around her to hug her against her side. "That's a big decision, but I think if you tell your Papa what you're thinking and what you're feeling, he'll listen to reason. If it were just up to me, I'd say sure, stay here with us, but it's not my decision alone." She could feel the tension leave the girl's shoulders under her embrace. "What about your grandparents? Would they be okay with this?"

"I think so," Janissa replied. "I overheard Memaw saying she couldn't wait until I went back to school so she could rest. She didn't mean it in a bad way, but I know it's hard for them."

"Let's go talk to Chase now, shall we?" Cassidy asked.

"What if he says no?" Janissa bit her lip and looked down at her lap. She didn't want to show her suddenly watery eyes.

"Then we'll figure out a compromise of some kind. Come on, let's go catch him while he's relaxing."

Chase knew he was in it when he saw the two most important women in his life walk into the room holding hands. "Ladies?" he rumbled with a faint smile on his lips. "What do I need to fix now?"

Janissa let go of Cassidy's hand and ran to him to give him a hug where he sat on the couch. "Papa, it's time. I want to stay here with you and Cassidy. Memaw and

Pops are getting old and I feel lonely a lot when I'm at school."

Chase kept an arm around her as she settled beside him, then looked up at Cassidy as she took a seat on the coffee table across from him. "What's your take on this?"

"Nissa and I had a chat and she let me know how she's been feeling and her worries about her grandparents – and I told her we had to ask you. That it wasn't a decision I could make for her." She paused and looked at the hopeful expression on Nissa's face, then looked back at Chase. "However, I'm all for her staying here, attending her current school online or looking at local schools if that's preferred. We're building a family, you and I – and she's part of it. I think we should all build it together."

Chase turned to Janissa and lifted her chin with his fingers to meet her gaze. "This is a big step, Nissa. It's a lot of adjustment for all of us. I'll need you to really put in the work to make this a good thing, yeah?"

"I want to make it a good thing," Janissa told him, as her body quivered with excitement. "I've wanted to be a family again for a long time."

"Is that why you brought so much stuff?" Chase asked her with a grin.

"I brought stuff to decorate my room, like you said," Nissa sniffed. "And I've already put most of my things at home in boxes. I don't have any stuff at school because they're working on the dorms so I had to bring it all home anyway. That's why I thought about the online classes because we're all online for a few weeks while they fix the buildings."

"You had a lot of hope that your plan would work," Cassidy told the girl as she reached for your hand. "Sometimes, that's all we can do. Put in the work and hope it pays off."

Then Janissa showed a wisdom beyond her years as she looked at Cassidy. "Are you going to be okay with being my mom? I had a mama, and she's been gone a long time. You're not replacing her, you're being something else. A mom, not a mama. Does that even make sense?" she mused after a moment.

Cassidy had to swallow a sudden lump in her throat. She'd wanted a family of her own all of her life, but had given up hope that it would ever happen after Everett. She'd decided to put her energy into her career and her community and put the rest behind her. "Yes, that makes a lot of sense. I'd love to be your mom, Janissa. But you're going to have to be patient with me. I've never been a mom before and I'll have to figure it out as I go."

"It's been a long time since I had a mother, so I'll probably need your patience, too," Janissa replied, then gave Cassidy a hug. "Thank you," she whispered near Cassidy's ear. "Thank you so much."

Chase watched the two of them and felt his heart burst with love. "I'm the luckiest man alive right now," he rumbled. "And I've got some work to do. Janissa, I'll call your grandparents and discuss things with them, and get the school information updated. Do you have your tablet and monitor with you, or do we need to get them sent right away?"

"I've got them with me. I'm working on an extra credit report with Monique over the break, so I had to bring it," Nissa said. "And you already got me a cool desk, so I'll just set it all up there."

"Why don't you go finish settling in? Cassidy and I need to work out how to get everything handled," Chase told her.

"Okay, Papa," Nissa replied as she bounced to her feet. "Thank you, Mom," she told Cassidy and raced down the hall to her room.

Cassidy held it together until the bedroom door shut, then she slid into Chase's lap and wound her arms around him. "I'm a *mom*."

"Yes, my love, you most definitely are. Thank you for welcoming her into your heart. It means everything to me," Chase whispered against her hair. He held her for a few minutes, then leaned back and looked at her face. "What do we do with her when we're both working?"

"Good question. Guess we've got a lot to figure out," Cassidy said with a wry laugh.

"Best get to it, then," Chase said and reached for his tablet.

Myke watched Agent Winslow take a seat next to Red at the console and her mouth went dry. She was supposed to be listening and contributing, but all she could do was stare at Fee and remember.

"Mykal," Red said. "Are you with us?"

"Sorry, Red. Lost in thought. Are we thinking Bentley's running or just hiding out and waiting for something?" Myke said.

"Or a little of both," Ophelia said. She glanced over at Myke, then turned her attention to the screens. Redmond Jefferson was a legend and she could handle being in proximity to Mykal Cutler if it meant she got to work with Red. "The file from Univy that FBIS received has given us enough to supplement what Agent Cutler had already discovered, that there's a warrant for his immediate arrest, no matter where in the universe he surfaces."

"About fucking time," Red muttered. "If the powers that be had listened when we first came up with the information, my family wouldn't have nearly been killed."

"I heard about the attack on Ms. Foster," Ophelia said. "I'm glad no one was injured." She smoothed a hand over her auburn curls and tucked a clip more firmly into place.

When unbound, Fee's hair brushed mid-back, but she wore it braided and pinned in a crown around her head. Some of the soft curls escaped and brushed skin of a delicate porcelain hue that bore a faint dusting of freckles across her cheeks and the bridge of her nose. Dark green eyes that glinted with intelligence caught Myke's gaze in the reflection of a dark screen before they quickly looked away.

"Miz Lacey is working in the other room, if you have any questions for her," Myke said. "But she's doing fine. Red's making sure she stays close until Grant can get the car fixed up."

"If Grant hadn't bought that car for her, they'd all be dead," Red said as he pulled up another report. "Okay, if we can focus, this is where we've got with the plan to find Bentley so far."

Both agents turned their focus to Red and they got to work. Bentley had to be stopped and soon, but they had no idea where to start looking.

Chapter Twenty-Seven

It took a couple of hours, but soon Chase and Cassidy had handled the arrangements for getting Janissa settled with them permanently. The grandparents were relieved and thrilled she'd be back with Chase – and they couldn't wait to meet Cassidy. They said they'd even arrange to have the rest of Janissa's things packed up and shipped to Chase. The school situation was simply an adjustment of addresses – there would be no interruption in her classes.

Once they'd taken care of that much, Cassidy suggested she pack up a lunch and the three of them take a short hike to the waterfall that fed into Bear Creek. Red's property straddled Bear Creek with his home on one side and the village across a driving bridge on the other. There were trails all through the forest that led off the property and into a state preserve, which is where the waterfall could be found.

Each wore a backpack with water, protein bars, a basic medical kit, dry socks, and so on, while Chase also had the lunch in his pack. Each had a folding knife in a pocket or on their belt and while Chase wore long pants, the ladies wore cargo-style shorts and t-shirts with sweatshirts tied around their waists. It was warm enough now to not need them, but it would be cooler at the falls. All three had well-worn hiking boots and Janissa had found a cap and pulled her braids through the hole in the back to keep them up off of her neck.

They walked down the road to the bridge, then took the trail that wound along the creek. The weather was perfect for a hike with that late summer warmth and clear blue skies. The scent of pine nearly overpowered the mossy scent of the creek as it bubbled beside them.

"Just so you know, Nissa, your grandparents are thrilled that we're staying together and they'll pack up the remainder of your things and ship them up here," Chase told her as they walked. "They also told me that this was ideal because things had become more difficult for them as they got older, and they were trying to figure out how to discuss some changes with me when you asked to stay." He reached out and tapped the bill of her cap. "Smart young lady, you made everyone more comfortable."

"I overheard them once saying how exhausting it was for them to have me home. I know they love me, but it was time for a change," Nissa replied. She paused to crouch near a cluster of bright red bee balm, the patch catching a spot of sunlight between the towering trees. A hummingbird dipped past Nissa's nose to feast and she barely breathed while the bird sampled the blooms.

"That was so mag," Nissa whispered as she got to her feet and hurried to catch up. "There's so much life in the forest," she said as they took an easy pace along the trail. "Squirrels and chipmunks and all kinds of birds are everywhere. They don't even hide when they hear us coming."

"That's because this trail is used often and they've adjusted to having people walk by," Cassidy told her. "Do you have an interest in plants or animals?"

"I have an interest in everything right now," Nissa told her. "My teachers tell us we should try a bit of everything and see which calls to us the most. We should explore all of the possibilities before picking one to study first."

"Those are wise teachers," Chase said. "Sometimes there are several interests in a person's life. They might start, like me, with sports and football, then look into the law and being a lawyer before settling on something like public service. I know I won't be a cop forever, but I enjoy it while I'm doing it now. I might want to look at designing security systems or perhaps go back into studying the law when I get older. There are so many possibilities out there, there's no need to lock yourself into just one."

As the trail rose up along the base of the ridge, they stopped talking and focused on where they put their feet. Chase led with Janissa in the middle and Cassidy behind as they wove through trees with roots jutting out over the top of the soil. Rocks gave hand and foot holds as the path grew steeper still until they leveled out and stopped at the first ledge. The creek was about twenty feet below them now and they could see the falls up ahead. Crystal clear water spilled over a ledge of rocks worn smooth from centuries of running water, splashing and spraying as it hit a series of ledges and outcroppings on the way down to the creek. Ferns and flowers grew in pockets where the water spray misted but didn't pound and when the sun shot through, a rainbow shimmered.

"This is beyond mag," Nissa whispered. "It's so beautiful." She lifted her wrist device and framed a few shots to enjoy later. "Are we going higher?"

"The next ledge up isn't that far and there are a couple of stone arrangements that make good places to sit and eat," Cassidy told her. "You up for more?"

"Most definitely," Nissa said and started up the trail.

Chase let her go ahead this time and reached for Cassidy's hand. "You're being wonderful with her."

"She's easy to be wonderful with," Cassidy told him, then leaned up to give him a kiss. "You take up the rear for a bit, hm?" A wink and she wiggled her hips before she followed Nissa up the trail.

Chase sighed and shook his head as he watched Cassidy's curvy backside climb the next patch of trail. "That woman's going to torture me for the rest of my days." He put his hands on his hips and grinned. "I'm so damned lucky."

They reached the next ledge and Chase handed Cassidy his pack at her request so she could unpack the lunch. Nissa blushed as she leaned in to Cassidy to whisper that she needed to relieve herself.

Cassidy took a moment to look around. "Those bushes over there. Thick enough for privacy and I don't see any prickly plants. You've got a bag and wipes in your pack."

Nissa gave her a nod and scurried off. Cassidy turned to Chase as he looked up and mouthed 'bio break' before he could embarrass the girl.

Sandwiches, chilled drinks, fresh fruit, and cookies for dessert were set out on the rock table. She put the container of cookies off to the side, then frowned and looked around. "She's taking too long," she muttered and turned to Chase. "Keep an eye on the food, I'll go check on Nissa."

Cassidy moved past a couple of trees and grew closer to the brush when she heard a hissed whisper and a soft cry of pain. She pulled her knife and edged around the larger clump of bushes and spotted Nissa held against a man she barely recognized as Folsom Bentley.

"I told you to stop struggling," Bentley hissed in Nissa's ear. "I've got a stunner right here." He held a rock in one hand that he jabbed into Nissa's side.

Cassidy snapped out the words as she rushed toward Bentley. "It's a rock, Nissa. Drop and roll!"

Nissa drove an elbow back into Bentley's ribs, turned in his grip and rammed a knee up towards his groin, but hit his thigh instead. Then she dropped out of his grasp and rolled out of reach before she pushed to her feet and raced towards Chase. "Papa! Help!"

Bentley roared and turned towards Cassidy, the rock raised in his fist.

Cassidy crouched with her hands at the ready, one with the knife blade along her forearm, the hilt in her fist. "Come on Bentley, you want to play with the girls? Try one of the big girls."

"I'm going to smash your head in and fuck your corpse," Bentley snarled. They circled around the clearing as they faced each other.

"Wow, that's not sexy at all," Cassidy taunted him. "You need a shower first. You're kind of disgusting there, bud. Been living rough for a few days?"

"Fucking cabin was barely a shack. No running water, nothing," Bentley whined. "I had to come get water at the creek."

"And you thought you'd just attack my daughter for shits and giggles?" Cassidy asked. "Pathetic."

"I'm not pathetic!" Bentley roared and rushed toward Cassidy.

The sound of a pulse weapon ripped through the forest and hit Bentley in the chest. His eyes went wide as he dropped to his knees. Chase came up beside Cassidy and put a hand on her arm. "You are magnificent," he told her as he kissed her cheek. "Would you go help Nissa while I wrap this fucker up with a bow?"

"No problem," Cassidy said as she gave Chase's arm a pat and turned back toward the lunch spot. Cassidy heard the roar before she got back to Nissa. She turned in time to see Bentley, his head buried in Chase's chest, his arms around his torso as Chase grabbed the man's hips and pulled upwards, then threw Bentley away from him.

Chase grabbed at his side where Bentley had stabbed him with a broken bottle he'd found in the brush, then stumbled over to where Bentley lay still on the ground. He held the stunner on Bentley in case he tried another surprise attack, then reached with his bloodied hand to check for a pulse.

He'd noticed the odd angle of Bentley's head in relation to his torso, so it didn't surprise him that there was no pulse. A nearby tree offered a crutch to pull himself to his feet and he turned as Cassidy rushed back to him.

"He's dead. He stabbed me with a broken bottle. Let's get away from the body before Nissa comes looking, okay?" Chase leaned on Cassidy as she led him back to the stones and their daughter.

Calm and efficient, Nissa clean the wound and helped to get Chase patched up enough for transport while Cassidy called Red and got a team out there to claim Bentley's body and process the scene.

"Not exactly the afternoon I had planned," Chase said as he watched Nissa tape the padding over the wound.

"Not in my plans either, Papa," Nissa told him. "This is going to need sealing and better cleaning. That bottle was probably ancient and buried in the muck for fifty years. It's only deep on one side, though."

"How'd you get so good at this?" Chase asked.

"Advanced first aid training in school. I've also advanced to brown belt in my combat training, so when Cassidy told me he didn't have a stunner, I fought back and got away."

Chase was so proud, he could barely speak. He reached up a hand to cup the back of her neck and touched his forehead to hers. "You're my treasure, little one. I'm so damned proud of you."

Nissa rested a hand on his forearm and kept her forehead bent to his. "You were always good at making the monsters go away. Now you've got a partner that's just as good at it. I'm a lucky girl."

"We're all lucky," Cassidy said as she approached the two of them. "A heli will drop in the clearing about fifty yards away. You up for a casual stroll, Chase?"

"With my two ladies? Always."

Chapter Twenty-Eight

Three days after Bentley's death, Red sat at the table with Chase and Cassidy. Nissa was down at the gym with Myke, training together. The two of them had become fast friends when Myke had told Nissa a few stories about Chase as a kid.

Red pulled out his tablet and swiped to put the images up on the screen. "The case against Bentley is solid but now that he's dead, it's all for show. We found four more young women frozen the lower level of Bentley's house, where he had freezer storage. Also, while we know Owens is likely the one that killed the first two men, everything currently points toward Bentley being the one who dropped all three bodies into the forest."

"We can't pin anything on Owens yet," Chase grumbled. "But that doesn't mean we're going to stop trying, correct?"

"Correct," Red replied. "We're just going to widen our net and keep a very close watch on that lab. The recorders you posted are now legally there with a secret warrant. While they keep telling us it's a medical research facility, we all know it's also going to be a drug production and processing center. It's up to us to build the case."

"Then that's what we'll do. You've said before," Cassidy told Red, "That these kinds of cases can take years. We'll stay on it as long as it takes."

"Speaking of years," Red said as he leaned back and shut down the screen. "There are some changes happening and I wanted to get your input."

Chase reached out and took Cassidy's hand, their attention on Red's face.

"Grant and Ellery are moving into their house this week," Red told them. "It's finally cleared for occupancy, even though a bunch of the cosmetic stuff isn't done. They're still trying to decide on paint for a few of the rooms, but they want to get settled and work on it while they live there."

"I don't see," Cassidy started to say and Chase gave her fingers a squeeze.

"Now you've got a teenager and a partner in your space, Chase, I think you could use a bit more room. Grant wants to take Ellery's pod and put it on their land for a guest cottage – and since he's paid for them all, I'm not inclined to argue. However, we got talking and realized we could add on to your structure and utilize the space from Elle's place, and give you all some room to spread out." Red paused and looked from one to the other. "Now, before we do that, though, I have to ask. Do you plan on staying here?"

Cassidy looked at Chase and gave him a faint nod, then he smiled and turned to Red. "We're staying. Janissa feels safe here, and with the enhanced security, I feel safe with her being here alone while we're working."

Red smiled at them both, then tapped his fingers on the table. "While she's old enough to stay on her own in a high security space, I've got another suggestion that you're welcome to take or discard as you wish."

They both looked at Red as he paused, then continued. "One of my agents needs a place to recuperate. He's physically and mentally sound enough to be released from medical, but he needs some time to figure out his next steps. His name is Hudson Hayes. He's thirty-four years old and has been an agent for nine years."

"You want this guy to be a caretaker for Janissa when we're not around?" Chase asked Red. "I trust your judgement, Red, but are you sure he's up for dealing with a teenage girl?"

"A highly intelligent, well-bred teenage girl," Red replied. "He needs a reason to move forward. His story

isn't really mine to tell, but suffice to say he lost everything - his home, his family, and almost his life. I was
going to have him come stay in Elle's place, but since
that's not possible now, we'll just shuffle a few things
around and give him a space on the other side of your
place. He'll be next door and convenient for Janissa if
she needs someone – and good for him to see a family
getting established after so much loss."

Cassidy looked over at Chase, then turned to Red. "We
can give it a shot. If it doesn't work out, he's still got
people around him and we'll figure something else out
for Nissa."

Chase gave a nod. "I hope you know what you're doing,
Uncle Red."

Red gave them a faint smile. "So do I."

Logan crossed the bridge over the creek and slowed as
the lights along the road gave him his first look at the
village. He followed Red's instructions and pulled into
the parking space in front of the first house on the right.
There were lights on inside and he shut off his truck and
went to knock before he brought anything inside. He
wanted to make sure it was the right place.

The door opened and Red stood there with a smile and his arms held wide. "Come here, Logan. Welcome home."

Logan finally felt welcomed for the first time since he'd packed up his things in Wilmington. He stepped into Red's embrace and returned it with a couple of pats on the back. His gaze went past Red to where Lacey Foster stood in the kitchen and his smile grew.

"Miz Lacey," he said as he moved to hug her as well. "You're both a sight for these tired eyes."

"We've been waiting for you," Lacey said. "We bought you some furniture and a few things to help you feel at home."

"Let's get your stuff inside," Red said. "Then Lacey can show you around and we can leave you to get settled."

"I made your favorite chicken pot pie in small casserole dishes so you could heat them up as you wished. There are a few things in the fridge and freezer, and one casserole in the oven, staying warm, so you can have a good hot meal tonight," Lacey told him once they'd brought in the few boxes and bags from the truck.

"She's got you set up for a few days, son. Just take some time and settle in. I'll swing by tomorrow to talk," Red said.

"Actually, I wanted to ask you something before I lose my nerve," Logan said to Red. "You know I've done consulting for the FBIS and some of the other agencies over the past few years, right?"

Red arched a brow and gave him a nod. "I'm aware of some of it, yes."

"I want a permanent job doing just that. No more Father Logan McMann. I'm just Dr. Logan McMann now, and I need work."

"Okay, then. Let me see what I can do and I'll come by tomorrow." Red paused and put a hand on Logan's shoulder. "I could use a psychiatrist with behavioral expertise on my team. For now, eat and rest and we'll talk tomorrow."

"Thank you, Uncle Red," Logan said with a weary smile. "And thank you, Miz Lacey. I feel like I'm home for the first time in a long while."

Lacey looped her arm through Red's as they walked back down the road to Red's place. "Think you can help that boy?"

"I know I can," Red said. "The question is, is he ready to help himself?"

Inside the neat cottage home, Logan locked the door and pulled his kit bag into the bathroom. He desperately needed a shower and to wash the miles off of him. Once clean, he pulled on cotton shorts and a t-shirt, then went to get the food Miz Lacey had left for him. A large glass of milk, a big bowl of chicken pot pie, and he sat at the table and looked around the space while he ate.

The gray sofa and blue chairs looked comfortable and inviting. The rug laid over plank floors was blue, gray, and cream stripes, and an old trunk served as a coffee table. He'd seen the dark blue comforter and crisp white sheets on the bed with a white and blue patterned rug on the floor. Everything was clean, comfortable, and just enough color that he could make it more his own without too much effort. He just hoped he could learn how to do that.

Logan hadn't had a home since he was a child. Oh, he'd had places he'd lived, but they weren't really his. This was the first place he'd been since he left his parent's house that he could, potentially, see as being a home he'd be happy to call his own.

First steps first, though. He needed a job, and he needed to let his friends know he was back and ready to help.

He just had to decide how much he was going to tell them.

THE END

Want more? Grab your copy of Bishop, the next book in the Chess Club Mystery Series. https://books2read.c om/chessclubBishop

Description:

Logan's blood family no longer spoke to him, but his chosen family had drawn him back to Lakeridge, North Carolina. As though fulfilling his promises to either would be easy.

He'd left Lakeridge after high school with only a few visits to his mother since then. Now he was moving back to help his friends figure out who had killed one of their own - Wes Davenport. Officiating the funeral had been one thing; leaving the priesthood and taking a job to help solve multiple mysteries was another.

It was time for Logan to go home and help his chosen family and pick up the pieces of his shattered heart. And maybe figure out who he really was.

About the Author

Bestselling author TK Eldridge retired from a career in Intelligence for the US Gov't to write. The experiences from then are now being used to feed the muse for romance, mysteries-thrillers, supernatural, paranormal, and whatever else captures their imagination.

TK Eldridge writes about all kinds of people because it is our variety as humans that makes us fascinating. Their hope is to encourage people to see the world differently through the character's eyes, and through the character's journey.

When they're not writing, they are enjoying life in the Blue Ridge mountains of western North Carolina. Two dogs, a garden, a craft hobby and a love of Celtic Traditional music keep them from spending too much time at the computer.

You can connect with them on:

Website: https://tkeldridge.com

BookBub: https://www.bookbub.com/profile/t-k-eldridge

Subscribe to their newsletter: https://tkeldridge.com/newsletter

Milton Keynes UK
Ingram Content Group UK Ltd.
UKHW040701250823
427479UK00004B/155